## She'd heard rumors of his engagement...

Yet Margot's heart lurched with a violence that made the earth seem to tilt as she caught sight of Jordan's tall, muscular figure approaching her.

"I never expected to see you here," she said nervously.

"Your mother told me where I'd find you." He glanced about him, taking in the willow trees stripped bare of their foliage, then his eyes fastened on hers with a strange intensity. "About the other night..." he began.

"I haven't given it a thought since," she lied desperately. "I've written that off to experience."

"Don't lie to me," he commanded. His hands slid down her arms to encircle her waist, and she was suddenly besieged with a mad desire to know again the touch of his lips....

# Books by Yvonne Whittal

# YVONNE WHITTAL

## where two ways meet

*Harlequin Books*

TORONTO • NEW YORK • LONDON
AMSTERDAM • PARIS • SYDNEY • HAMBURG
STOCKHOLM • ATHENS • TOKYO • MILAN

Harlequin Presents first edition September 1984
ISBN 0-373-10726-9

Original hardcover edition published in 1981
by Mills & Boon Limited

# CHAPTER ONE

THE news that Jordan Merrick was returning to South Africa, after spending seven fruitful years in Europe, spread with the swiftness of a fire warning throughout Willowmead, a small village situated in the heart of the wine-producing valleys of the Cape, but Margot Huntley heard it for the first time in the Willowmead Clinic's operating theatre where, as Theatre Sister, she was assisting Dr Daniel Grant while he delicately reconstructed the badly disfigured features of a patient who had been referred to him by a colleague in Cape Town.

Daniel Grant, a terse, clever man, seldom encouraged conversation in the operating theatre, but that particular day turned out to be an exception, and the conversation revolved around the expected arrival of the new man to fill the post of Senior Surgeon which had been vacant for some weeks, and at some point in the conversation Dr Grant looked up unexpectedly from his task.

'You should know him, Sister Huntley,' he said bluntly. 'It's Jordan Merrick.'

Margot faltered, but only for a fraction of a second before her long years of training came swiftly to her rescue, and she slapped the required instrument into Dr Grant's outstretched palm without anyone so much as noticing anything odd about her, but beneath her mask her lips had tightened and her mouth had gone peculiarly dry.

'Like most people in Willowmead I know of Jordan Merrick, but I don't know him personally,' Margot managed without a tremor in her soft, faintly husky voice.

Conversation dwindled abruptly after that as the operation progressed and became more intricate, and Margot thrust aside her disturbed thoughts to watch with interest and fascination as Daniel Grant's clever, skilled hands performed the ever-increasing miracles of surgery. It was several hours later, when she entered the small office allotted to the Theatre Sister, that she allowed herself to dwell on the subject of the new Senior Surgeon.

'Like most people in Willowmead I know of Jordan Merrick,' she recalled her own words, and she also recalled many other things she would rather have forgotten.

Jordan Merrick had been one of the most outstanding scholars Willowmead had ever produced. As an athlete, and captain of the school rugby team, he had earned himself the honour of having his name engraved on the brass plaques lining the walls of the foyer at Willowmead's small but illustrious school. Added to this, he had been extremely good-looking, and all the girls—including Margot—had at one time or another fallen for this tall, dark-haired Adonis with the magnificent physique.

Margot had been ten, and he a superior being of eighteen in his final year at school, when their paths had literally collided for the first time. She had been sent on an errand to one of the senior classes when, coming from opposite directions, they had rounded a corner simultaneously, and the impact had sent her spinning on to the gravel path. A spotless white handkerchief had been produced to dry her tears, then the expensive linen object had been dampened to gently remove the traces of gravel from her grazed knee, and she had worshipped him from the moment she had looked up into those dark, concerned eyes. He had been her hero, her idol, but, like most idols, he had tumbled from the pedestal where she had placed him, and her young heart had been crushed.

This had come about in the cruellest way. For more than half a century the railway line had split Willowmead's community into two distinct sections; a right side for the upper class families, and a wrong side for those who were less fortunate. The right side lay to the west at the foot of the mountain, while the wrong side lay eastwards towards the river, and not even on the school benches did the two sides mix socially with ease.

Margot lived on the wrong side of the tracks in a small, two-bedroomed house with a corrugated iron roof. She had lived there ever since she could remember. Her father had worked long, arduous hours for a meagre salary as an employee of the railways, but his earnings had paid the instalments on their home, and although there had never been funds for luxuries, there had always been enough to feed and clothe themselves until a shunting accident had ended his life when Margot was barely eight years old. A widow's pension secured the roof over their heads, but Margot's mother had been forced to fall back on her trade as a dressmaker in order to make ends meet financially.

Jordan Merrick had lived on the right side of the tracks. He was the only son of elderly parents, and although old Mr Merrick had died two years ago while Jordan was still away in Europe, Mrs Merrick still lived on in the enormous whitewashed mansion. They were of the cream of society, and Margot's mother had made many elaborate dresses for Mrs Merrick, who attended all the important functions, and Mrs Merrick seldom wore the same dress twice. Margot had done most of the deliveries for her mother and, as a result, she had occasionally caught a glimpse of Jordan during those years when he had been a medical student at Cape Town University.

Margot could still remember vividly the last time she had seen Jordan. She had been seventeen, while he, eight years her senior, had been in his final year at varsity. She had cycled up to the Merrick house to deliver a parcel of dresses, and Jordan had answered her knock on the heavy oak door. His usual smile of polite recognition had been replaced by a glowering stare when he had found her on the doorstep and, without relieving her of her heavy parcel, he had turned on his heel and strode off into a room leading off the spacious hall.

'It's that kid from the other side of town, and it surprises me, Mother, that you haven't yet told her we have a tradesman's entrance for people like her,' Margot had heard him say quite distinctly.

He had perhaps not realised that Margot would be able to hear his scathing remark, but his angry voice had carried and, hurt and bewildered, she had left the parcel on the small table just inside the door. She had cycled home in a blind fury; a fury which had devoured the hurt, as well as the tender feelings she had nurtured for him, and she had sworn afterwards never to set foot on Merrick soil again. She would have expected that sort of remark from his mother, but somehow she had thought Jordan different, and it had been a crashing blow to discover that her idol was, after all, a social snob like his mother, and several other families in the village.

Many of the social prejudices had died a natural
death during recent years with the influx of strangers to
this small valley town, but habit dies hard, and rebuffs
suffered as a child are seldom forgotten, with the result
that Margot remained withdrawn and wary of new
friendships outside her duties as Theatre Sister at the
clinic.

Dragging her thoughts back to the present, Margot
sighed and glanced at the watch pinned to her spotless
white uniform. It was time she went home and, draping
her dark blue cape about her slim shoulders, she picked
up her handbag, and left the office, closing the door
firmly behind her. In the passage she passed Dr Grant
on his way to the wards, and, without pausing, he inclined his head briefly in her direction.

As co-director, Chief Surgeon, and part owner of the
clinic, Dr Grant had won everyone's respect and admiration, and although his formidable, often abrupt
manner was a little frightening at times, Margot knew
that he cared a great deal for the comfort and welfare of
his patients, for he seldom left the clinic at night without paying an unscheduled visit to all his patients, re-
gardless of the time.

There were times when Margot felt sorry for his wife,
but Joanne Grant probably understood his concern
better than anyone else, considering that she had once
worked in the theatre with her husband.

Darkness came swiftly and early to the valley during
the winter months, and Margot drew her cape closer
about her to keep out the stinging cold as she hurried
out of the yellow brick building to where her small
green Mini was parked. Cypress, oak and chestnut trees
threw deeper shadows across the beautiful, spacious
gardens of the clinic which stood high up on the rise of

the mountain overlooking the vineyards in the valley below, but Margot gave her surroundings no more than a cursory glance as she began the ten-minute drive down the winding road towards the village.

Her thoughts returned to Joanne Grant and the year she had spent as Theatre Sister at the clinic before Dr Grant's arrival in Willowmead to take over from the deceased Dr van Amstel. She had been known as Joanne Webster then, but although she had remained coldly aloof from the rest of the staff, and something of a mystery, Margot had found her fair in her administrations as Theatre Sister. Within weeks of Dr Grant's arrival, however, the clinic had been literally agog with the news that Joanne was, in actual fact, the wife of the estimable Dr Daniel Grant, and had been so for almost eighteen months. Margot was still not sure why it had been kept such a secret, but she supposed Dr Grant and his wife had had their reasons. During the three years which had elapsed since then, Margot had met Joanne Grant occasionally at staff functions, but instead of being cold and aloof, Margot had found her warm, friendly and sincere.

She was not, however, thinking of Joanne Grant when she arrived at her home and parked her car in the single garage beside the house. She was thinking of Jordan Merrick, and his return to Willowmead was, strangely enough, one of the first things her mother discussed with her the moment Margot entered the house through the kitchen door.

'I hear that Jordan Merrick is coming back to work at the clinic,' said Beryl Huntley, and Margot glanced at her in mild surprise.

'Someone has been quick off the mark, it seems,' she observed dryly.

'You know about it, then?' her mother questioned almost accusingly.

'I heard this afternoon.' Margot stared at the small, frail woman seated in the chair beside the well-scrubbed table, and frowned curiously. 'Who told you?'

'Phyllis Green,' Beryl Huntley smiled mischievously. 'She had tea with me this afternoon.'

Margot snorted angrily. 'Since young Betsy has been working at the Post Office her mother has become a veritable mine of information, and if Phyllis doesn't watch her step, she might find that her daughter will be without a job one of these days!'

Beryl Huntley nodded in agreement and changed the subject. 'Eva Merrick must be tremendously happy at the thought of having her son home to stay.'

'I presume so,' Margot replied noncommittally.

'He was always such a nice boy, and always so courteous.'

'He's a Merrick,' Margot reminded her mother sharply.

'That may be so, but you thought a lot of him once,' Beryl Huntley remarked, eyeing her daughter thoughtfully. 'What changed your mind?'

'I grew up,' Margot replied scathingly, dropping her cape and her handbag on to a chair and helping herself to a cup of coffee. She drank it black with only a little sugar, and while she did so she observed her mother over the rim of her cup.

Beryl Huntley was greying swiftly and had lost a considerable amount of weight over the past months. The grey eyes, so like Margot's, lacked their usual lustre, and the work-roughened hands lay idly on the table before her. Those hands had often worked the long hours through the night, the fingers nimble as they stitched and sewed with expert precision in order to have the required garments ready on time for delivery, and the money earned from this often ungrateful task had paid for Margot's education and other necessary items such as food and clothing. Margot's salary as a student nurse at Willowmead's general hospital had eased the strain on her mother a great deal, but it was only since she had joined the staff at the clinic four years ago that her salary had been sufficient enough to alleviate the necessity for her mother to work.

Looking at her mother now with a critical, clinical eye, she realised that those years of hard work and deprivation had taken their toll, and it filled her with deep concern.

'When do you have to see Dr Turner again?' she asked, and her mother gestured evasively with her hands.

'At the end of the month,' Beryl grimaced as if she found the thought distasteful.

'You shouldn't work so hard, Mum,' Margot said anxiously, rinsing her cup in the kitchen sink. 'I could quite easily come home in the evenings and see to the dinner.'

'Nonsense!' Beryl exclaimed indignantly. 'You're on your feet all day in the theatre, and I won't have you coming home in the evenings to slave over a hot stove!'

'You need to rest more.'

'I rest enough,' her mother insisted, brushing aside Margot's concern with a laugh. 'It's laziness,' she added. 'It comes with old age sometimes.'

There was no answering smile on Margot's lips as she studied her mother thoughtfully. She was not at all convinced, but she laid the table without further comment before going down the passage to bath and change into something more comfortable before dinner.

Jordan Merrick's arrival at the clinic a few days later caused quite a stir among the nursing staff. Matron Selby, too, seemed to be having difficulty in controlling the rise and fall of her large bosom beneath the blue starched uniform when she and Dr Grant entered Margot's office early the morning with the new Senior Surgeon in tow.

He had changed considerably over the years, Margot decided, rising stiffly to her feet as she swiftly calculated his age at thirty-two. His chiselled, handsome features had hardened attractively, but it was that aura of authority about him which impressed her most of all despite her antagonistic feelings towards him.

Matron Selby made the introductions, and Margot's mouth suddenly went dry as if her salivary glands had stopped functioning when a strong, slender-fingered hand gripped hers briefly. She need not have been afraid to meet his glance, for those dark eyes looked down into hers without recognition, and she was grateful for it at that moment while she fought to control that odd flutter in her breast.

'Dr Merrick will spend the first few days acquainting himself with the various cases before being scheduled to operate, Sister Huntley, and I trust that you will assist him in the theatre as admirably as you do everyone else,' Dr Grant remarked and, for some reason, it sounded to Margot almost as if he had sensed her antagonism towards the new Senior Surgeon, and was issuing a warning.

'I shall do my best, as always, Dr Grant,' she said at once, stiffening with a measure of resentment.

The Chief Surgeon inclined his dark head and marched out of the small office with Matron Selby following close on his heels. Jordan Merrick, however, hesitated briefly before accompanying them, almost as if something about the Theatre Sister puzzled him, but the steady regard of her cool grey eyes told him nothing, and he turned on his heel moments later to follow the others down the passage.

Margot, admittedly, felt shaky after his departure, but the rest of the theatre staff were arriving, and there was plenty to do before they could start with the operations scheduled for that morning.

She did not look forward to working with Jordan Merrick, but a few days later, while assisting him in the theatre, she found him easy to follow despite the fact that his methods differed vastly from the others, and she watched with growing respect and admiration while those slim fingers did the first of several operations to repair the scarred tissue on a young woman's features.

When the patient was finally wheeled out of the theatre, Jordan pulled down his mask and turned towards Margot.

'I must compliment you, *and* your staff, Sister Huntley,' he said with a smile. 'It was a pleasure working under such organised conditions in such an organised theatre.'

'Thank you, Dr Merrick,' Margot replied stiffly, returning at once to her task of checking the instrument tray.

He seemed to linger at her side, but she ignored this, and moments later he turned away and walked out of the theatre. There was a titter among the two nurses assigned to theatre duty when the doors closed behind Jordan Merrick's tall, imposing frame, and Margot looked up to find the two girls almost swooning on their feet.

'Oh, Sister Huntley, isn't he divine,' Amy Barker, the eldest of the two sighed ecstatically while rolling her eyes dramatically towards the ceiling. 'I'd gladly cut myself just to have him touch me.'

Margot smiled inwardly, but her grey eyes beneath the dark, winged brows remained cool as she regarded her assistants steadily, but it was the senior nurse whom she addressed. 'Figuratively speaking, Barker, it's your throat which will be cut if this theatre is not shipshape when Matron comes round to inspect it in half an hour.'

'Oh, gosh!' Amy Barker nudged the girl next to her. 'Let's get a move on, June.'

Margot checked the instrument tray once more before leaving the theatre and returning to her office to write up her log book. Matron Selby arrived, as expected, precisely a half hour later, and Margot accompanied her on her weekly inspection tour of the theatre which had been left spotless by the two girls.

It was after five that afternoon when Margot finally returned to her office, and she had barely settled down to writing up her log book when a movement at the door made her look up to find Jordan Merrick's large frame dwarfing the entrance to her office. The jacket of his dark suit was unbuttoned, and his hands were thrust deep into the pockets of his pants.

'Forgive me for disturbing you, but——' He paused, and his dark eyes probed hers as he approached her desk. She rose respectfully to her feet, but he gestured her back into her chair and seated himself on the corner of her desk. 'I have a feeling that we've met somewhere before,' he said suddenly. 'Am I right?'

Margot felt ill at ease beneath the frowning intensity of his glance, but she answered politely, and without hesitation. 'My mother used to sew for Mrs Merrick.'

'Ah, yes, now I remember.' His brow cleared and a smile lurked in those fine dark eyes. 'You also used to work behind the counter in Solly Cohen's shop on Saturday mornings and during school holidays for pocket money.'

It surprised her that he should have remembered that, but his remark also annoyed her, and she said tritely, 'That "pocket money", as you call it, Dr Merrick, often provided my mother and me with the much-needed necessities every month.'

His smile vanished, and the chiselled features hardened. 'I meant no offence.'

'I'm sure you didn't, Dr Merrick,' she replied with a hint of sarcasm in her usually soft voice, then she brought an end to the conversation by indicating the open book before her. 'If you don't mind, I have this report to write up before I can go home.'

'Certainly,' he said at once, rising to his feet, and dwarfing her small office with the height and breadth of him. 'See you tomorrow, Sister Huntley.'

Margot found difficulty in concentrating on her work after his departure, and consequently it took her much longer to complete her report than she had anticipated. It was almost six o'clock when she drove her Mini through the gates of the clinic, but she had barely taken the first turn along the winding road towards the village when she caught sight of a white Mercedes in her rear view mirror. It approached her with speed and she moved over a little more to her side of the road to give it room to pass, but it remained directly behind her all the way down into the village. In the dusky light she was unable to recognise the driver, and neither did she know the car, but she found it more than a little nerve-racking when she crossed the bridge over the railway line and found that the Mercedes was still following close behind her. It was still there when she turned in at her gate, but it was gone when she had parked the Mini. Puzzled, her glance searched the quiet, empty street with its row of neat little houses overlooking the elec-trified railway line, then she shrugged and went inside out of the cold.

During dinner that evening Beryl Huntley asked in-quisitively, 'Have you seen him yet?'

'Have I seen whom?' Margot asked, keeping a straight face.

'Don't be dense, Margot,' her mother said impati-ently. 'You know very well that I'm referring to Jordan Merrick.'

Margot suppressed a smile. 'I've seen him, yes.'

'Has he changed much?'

'He's a little older, naturally,' Margot replied dryly. 'Pass the salt, please, Mum.'

'I wish you'd stop behaving in such an infuriating manner!' her mother accused as the salt exchanged hands.

'I'm sorry.'

'Well?' Beryl Huntley questioned when the silence had lengthened and stretched into minutes. 'Aren't you going to tell me about him?'

'Mum, there's nothing to tell,' Margot sighed, lower-ing her fork. 'I worked with him for the first time in the theatre this afternoon, and I think he's an excellent sur-geon. What more is there to tell you?'

Her mother smiled at her across the table. 'Did he talk to you?'

'Briefly, yes,' Margot nodded. 'May we step off the subject of Jordan Merrick now, please? It gives me indigestion.'

Beryl Huntley stared at her daughter curiously, but she did not pursue the subject, and made a half-hearted attempt at eating her food. Her plate, however, left the table practically untouched and, when Margot was about to voice her concern, Beryl forestalled her hastily by saying, 'Joanne Grant was here just after five this afternoon.'

Margot's eyes widened as a shock of surprise rippled through her. 'Dr Grant's wife?' she asked incredulously.

'I know of no other Joanne Grant, do you?' her mother smiled indulgently.

'Stupid question,' Margot agreed, helping herself to a cup of coffee. 'What did she want?'

'She didn't say,' her mother shrugged. 'She wanted to see you, but when you were so long in coming home she had to rush off home to see to her baby.'

'Didn't she give you any idea what it was about?' Margot asked, curious now to find out why Joanne Grant should have gone out of her way to come and see her at her home.

'No idea at all,' her mother replied. 'We had coffee, and chatted, but when she saw how late it was getting she left.'

'How strange,' Margot muttered to herself as she sat staring down into her cup of black, sweetened coffee in which the kitchen light danced crazily.

'She's such a lovely person, and so totally unaffected by the position her husband holds in this sometimes warped society of ours,' Beryl Huntley remarked. 'She wouldn't hear of going through to the lounge, and we sat here in the kitchen drinking our coffee.'

There was nothing wrong with having coffee in the kitchen with its bright, flowery curtains, its neat white cupboards, and scrubbed table, Margot thought confusedly. It was, in fact, the room where they had all their meals since there was no separate dining-room, but the thought of Joanne Grant being entertained in that very room seemed totally wrong, and she could not somehow picture the Chief Surgeon's wife making herself at home around the kitchen table.

She sighed and pushed a hand through her russet-coloured hair which hung loose down to her shoulders now that she was not in uniform. She was not ashamed of her home; she was, in fact, fiercely proud of it, but the entire incident puzzled her, and she was still thinking about it long after she had gone to bed that night.

Margot received an explanation for Joanne Grant's odd behaviour the following morning. She had barely had time to hang up her cape when the telephone on her desk started ringing, and she answered it unsuspectingly to find the Senior Surgeon's wife on the line.

'I'm glad I caught you before you have to go into the theatre,' Joanne told Margot. 'I was hoping to speak to you personally, that's why I called round at your home late yesterday afternoon, but now, I'm afraid, the telephone will have to do.' There was a brief pause, then she explained, 'I'm arranging a small welcoming dinner party at my home for Dr Merrick tomorrow evening, and I would like you to come.'

Margot's stomach muscles jerked into a knot. She hated having to refuse Joanne Grant, but the very thought of mixing with Willowmead's elite made her cringe inwardly, and she said a little too abruptly, 'I'm afraid I can't make it, Mrs Grant.'

'Oh, Margot, don't say that!' Joanne protested with

obvious disappointment in her voice.

'I'm sorry.'

'There's no one else I could invite, and I very much wanted you here,' she explained, surprising Margot. 'Couldn't you postpone your other engagement?'

Grasping at Joanne's supposition that she had another engagement, Margot said stubbornly, 'I'm afraid it's out of the question.'

'Oh.' Joanne seemed at a loss for words momentarily, then she said: 'Oh, well . . . if you should change your mind . . .'

'I'm sorry, Mrs Grant,' Margot said apologetically, feeling peculiarly as if she had let down an old friend.

'So am I,' Joanne replied with genuine sincerity, pausing almost as if she hoped Margot would still change her mind, then she said hastily, 'Ask my husband to give me a ring when he has a free moment this morning, will you?'

'I'll do that,' Margot promised, replacing the receiver on its cradle when the conversation ended abruptly.

She stood for a moment staring down at the instrument in thoughtful silence, then she sighed and studied the list of scheduled operations for the day. Dr Grant was not listed for an operation that morning and, lifting the receiver, she asked the switchboard to put her through to his office, but she was told promptly that Dr Grant was in consultation with Dr Ellis, the Senior Director and co-owner of the clinic, and it left Margot with no alternative but to pass on the message that he should contact his wife during the course of the morning.

Margot had no time after that to give Joanne Grant's invitation further thought. She was on her feet for the rest of the morning assisting Jordan Merrick with a very delicate operation which Dr Grant had assigned to him, and she was relieved when it was over, leaving her with enough time to relax over a leisurely lunch in the canteen.

She helped herself to a few salads and a cup of tea, and found herself a table in the corner beside a window which gave her an excellent view of the steeply terraced gardens and the valley below. It was an exceptionally warm winter's day with not a cloud in the sky, but she knew that with sunset the cold would set in to leave the valley white with frost the following morning. It was going to be a long winter, everyone had predicted, but on a sunny day such as this she could almost believe that spring was near.

She dragged her glance reluctantly from the scene outside and settled down to her lunch. The canteen was emptying swiftly, and Margot, too, was in a hurry to return to her duties some minutes later when she stacked her plates in the tray and rose to her feet.

'Leaving already, Sister Huntley?' a deep, familiar voice enquired, and she looked up to see Dr Grant approaching her table with a cup in his hand.

'I have a few things to check up on before afternoon surgery,' she explained, but he waved an authoritative hand towards the chair she had just vacated.

'Sit down,' he ordered abruptly. 'I never enjoy drinking my coffee alone.'

When the Chief Surgeon speaks one has to obey, and habit dies hard, she thought with a flicker of amusement as she cautiously seated herself opposite him. She felt more than just a little out of place as she sat there watching him drink his coffee, but her curiosity finally got the better of her.

'Forgive me for saying so, Dr Grant,' she began hesitantly, 'but it's rather unusual for you to be supporting the canteen during the lunch hour.'

'Hm . . .' His extraordinary blue eyes smiled at her across the table. 'What's that old saying about a change being as good as a holiday?'

Margot did not reply; she was, to say the least, at a loss for words as she sat there, but she could not help noticing that he glanced over his shoulder from time to time.

'Are you expecting someone, Dr Grant?' she asked eventually, and was surprised to hear him laugh.

'Look, Sister Huntley, I've never been very good at playing games, so I might as well admit that my wife talked me into delaying you, and . . .' a small blue Austin, familiar to Margot, swung into the parking area close to the canteen, and he relaxed visibly, 'here she is now.'

Margot stiffened automatically, but her glance was admiring as it followed the tall, slim young woman who climbed out of her car and walked the short distance from the parking area to the canteen. Her step seemed light, and the sun turned the shoulder-length brown hair to gold. Daniel Grant had been observing his wife as well, Margot noticed, and his usually stern features had softened briefly in a way she had never seen before.

Joanne disappeared from sight and, moments later, she was entering the canteen through the swing doors. She paused briefly, her glance sliding across the room, then she saw them, and a smile lit her face as she made her way quickly towards them among the unoccupied tables.

'I'm sorry I took so long, Daniel. I was held up at the last minute, and——' She halted abruptly, pulling up a chair to sit down while she glanced from her husband to

Margot and back again. 'Is something wrong?' she asked the stern-featured man seated at the table with them.

'I'm afraid I told Sister Huntley you asked me to delay her.'

'Oh, dear!' Joanne laughed selfconsciously.

'If it's about tomorrow evening, Mrs Grant, then you're wasting your time,' Margot informed her, rising to her feet and preparing to leave.

'I think I'll leave the two of you to battle it out on your own,' Dr Grant announced, giving his wife an 'I told you so' look as he got to his feet and squeezed her shoulder briefly. 'See you later, darling.'

Margot was about to follow him when Joanne, a couple of inches taller than herself, barred her way. 'I'm sorry, Margot,' she said, her soft green eyes apologetic as she placed her hand lightly on Margot's arm. 'Please . . . won't you sit down again?'

Margot relented, her liking and respect for this woman dictating her actions, but when they sat facing each other across the small table, Margot knew that she had to make Joanne Grant understand that her plight was useless.

'Mrs Grant——'

'Joanne,' the woman who was four years Margot's senior interrupted with a warm, persuasive smile. 'We've known each other long enough, surely, for you to drop the "Mrs Grant" nonsense?'

Margot shook her head. 'I appreciate the fact that you thought to invite me to dinner tomorrow evening, but I'm afraid my answer is still the same.'

Green eyes regarded Margot with an unnerving steadiness she remembered so well from the days when Joanne Grant had been Theatre Sister at the clinic, and she a third-year nurse.

'You're not allowing all those age-old prejudices to affect your decision, are you?'

Joanne's shrewdness did not surprise Margot, and without lowering her gaze, she said stiffly, 'I may work on the right side of the tracks, Mrs Grant, but I don't belong in your society.'

Margot regretted her remark instantly when Joanne Grant's face bore the look of someone who had been slapped, but she recovered swiftly although her smile was tinged with sadness.

'My name is Joanne to my friends,' she reminded Margot, 'and I'm sorry you feel that way about it, because, you see, I don't come from a wealthy family either. My father was a clerk in the Civil Service, and my brother and I were left destitute when my parents died unexpectedly, leaving us with no option but to throw ourselves at the mercy of others for our education.' She paused, her eyes growing misty with memories, then she laughed a little unsteadily and added, 'After a confession like that you must admit that I certainly don't qualify for the society in which you've placed me.'

One of the nicest things about Joanne Grant was the soothing warmth of her well-modulated voice, and although Margot did not quite understand the reason for this enlightening confession, she had found it pleasant just to listen to her.

'Why have you told me this?' Margot asked at last, and a great deal of mischief lurked in Joanne's smile.

'I'm hoping you'll agree to keep me company tomorrow evening.'

Why this calm, self-assured woman should need someone like herself to keep her company was beyond

Margot's understanding as she said protestingly, 'But you'll have your husband there with you.'

'Daniel is the dearest and the most wonderful man, but men are a breed entirely unto themselves,' Joanne replied laughingly, then she sobered, and her green eyes held an unmistakable plea in their depths. 'Will you come? For my sake? Or do you really have a prior engagement?'

Margot lowered her glance to her hands in her lap, and sighed. 'You're making it very difficult for me to refuse.'

'Good!' Joanne exclaimed hopefully. 'You'll come, then?'

There was no escape now, and raising her glance, Margot said helplessly, 'Yes, I'll come.'

'Wonderful!' Joanne exclaimed once again with obvious delight. 'You have a car, I know, so can we expect you at seven tomorrow evening?'

Margot nodded. 'I'll be there.'

'Thank you,' Joanne whispered, but as she rose to her feet she added hastily, 'I almost forgot—it's an informal dinner party, Margot. Nothing elaborate.'

Margot stared after her elegantly dressed figure with the feeling that she had agreed to something which she might yet live to regret, but if she had learnt anything from this meeting with the Chief Surgeon's wife, then it was the discovery that Joanne Grant had come from an ordinary home like her own, and that, despite her marriage to an eminent and wealthy surgeon, she had remained totally unpretentious.

# CHAPTER TWO

MARGOT was filled with misgivings when she arrived at the Grant home the following evening, but the lights were on in the two-storeyed mansion, and they beckoned welcomingly as she parked her Mini in the driveway. It was a cold night, and she shivered, drawing her coat more firmly about her as she stepped from the car and hurried up the steps towards the front door.

'Margot!' Joanne exclaimed moments later, smiling broadly as she extended both hands welcomingly towards Margot to draw her inside. 'Give me your coat and come and warm yourself by the fire.'

Margot slipped out of her coat, and while Joanne disposed of it she glanced about her nervously. The spacious hall was empty except for an antique bench, and a rosewood wall table on which stood a decorous arrangement of dried proteas. There was a curious lack of voices coming from the rooms leading off the hall and, turning to Joanne, she asked anxiously, 'Am I too early?'

'No,' Joanne shook her head and smiled. 'I thought you might find it easier to arrive before the others, instead of afterwards.'

'Joanne . . .' Margot began haltingly, unable to think of anything to say for a moment, then she asked slowly, 'Why are you being so kind to me?'

'I don't consider what I'm doing a kindness, but if you must have a reason, then let's say it's because

Daniel maintains that you're an excellent Theatre Sister, and in that capacity it's only right that you should be here. And because . . .' She tilted her head at a slight angle to observe Margot's straight-backed, slender figure, and a faraway look entered her eyes. 'I see myself in you sometimes; proud, fiercely independent, and nearly always on the defensive when you feel your existence is being threatened.'

Margot's throat felt constricted. Joanne Grant had far more understanding than she had credited her with, she thought, smiling a little shakily. 'Where's that fire? I'm cold,' she announced, feeling very much more at ease than she did a few moments ago.

'Right this way,' Joanne laughed, linking her arm through Margot's and leading her into the living-room where a wood fire crackled lustily in the grate.

'Ah, Margot,' Dr Grant greeted her, dropping his formal 'Sister Huntley' for the first time since she had known him as he uncurled his lean length from an armchair, and there was a hint of laughter in his eyes as he added, 'I'm delighted you decided to come.'

Margot suspected that he was mocking his wife in a subtle way, but Joanne seemed to take it in her stride as she smiled across at him and said: 'Pour the girl a drink, darling. She's frozen.'

'What will it be, Margot?' he asked, crossing the room towards the tall oak cabinet. 'A glass of our famous valley wine?'

'Yes, please, Dr Grant,' Margot replied, following Joanne's example and moving closer to the stone fireplace to warm herself. Seated, eventually, with a glass of wine in her hand, she looked about her appreciatively.

The living-room was simply and tastefully furnished

in restful shades of cream, gold and green, and everything about it, including the landscape in oils above the stone fire-place, suggested peace and tranquillity.

'You have a lovely home,' she said at last with her usual sincerity. 'This room looks as if it was made to relax in.'

'I have Joanne to thank for that,' Daniel Grant replied, a faint smile alleviating the sternness of his lean features. 'She's made this house a home, and a place to relax in after the strenuous hours in the operating theatre.'

'That's the nicest compliment you've paid me in a long time, Daniel,' Joanne remarked, her green eyes sparkling with teasing humour as they met his frowning observation.

'I'm not a man of many words, Lorelei, and you know that I speak only the truth.'

'Lorelei?' Margot repeated in an intrigued voice before she could prevent herself. 'That's an unusual name,' she added self-consciously.

There was a certain intimacy in the look that passed between husband and wife before Daniel Grant explained, 'Joanne reminded me of a sea nymph once, and the name has proved to be apt.'

Margot was surprised to see Joanne blush, but the tantalising conversation ended there at the sound of a car coming up the drive.

The first to arrive was the semi-retired Senior Director, Dr Ellis, and his wife. Dr Ellis, who had been persuaded to stay on at the clinic in an administrative capacity, was in a jovial mood, while his wife radiated a motherly warmth and charm which set Margot's nerves at ease.

The rest of the guests arrived soon afterwards, but

Margot felt that she could cope with Dr Neil Harris, the anaesthetist, as well as Matron Selby and her husband, George, who was the principal of the local school. It was the arrival of Jordan Merrick that troubled her most, and when he eventually entered the house accompanied by his mother, Margot felt her stomach muscles bunching themselves up into an uncomfortable knot.

Tall, and devastatingly attractive in a well-cut evening suit, Jordan seemed to dominate the living-room for her with his presence, and when those dark, compelling eyes met Margot's briefly, she felt an unfamiliar stirring within her breast which left her feeling oddly breathless. A warmth stole into her cheeks, and she lowered her eyes swiftly to listen with forced attentiveness to Neil Harris and Dr Ellis discussing the latest surgical equipment on the market.

It was while they were drinking a before dinner aperitif that Margot found Joanne and herself facing Eva Merrick, and Margot felt a tremor of acute nervousness pass through her as Jordan's mother appraised her with that familiar haughtiness in her bearing.

'I'd like you to meet a friend of mine,' Joanne announced, sliding her arm through Margot's. 'I don't suppose an introduction is really necessary, but I'd like you to meet Margot Huntley. You know Mrs Merrick, of course, Margot.'

'We have met before, yes,' Margot managed in a husky whisper.

'Huntley? Huntley?' Eva Merrick repeated embarrassingly, frowning slightly as she strove for recognition.

'My mother used to sew for you, Mrs Merrick,' Margot prodded her memory.

'Oh!' Eva Merrick's aristocratic features suddenly became cemented into a line of disapproval. 'Oh, yes, of course. You do still live on the other side of town, don't you?'

Margot felt like an object which had been catalogued and labelled unsuitable, but she raised her chin with a hint of defiance and said proudly, 'Yes, I do, Mrs Merrick.'

The silver-haired woman cast a final disparaging glance in Margot's direction, then she turned towards Joanne and said icily, 'May I know what this girl is doing here this evening?'

Bitterness rose within Margot until she could taste it in her mouth, but Joanne's swift reply stilled the words that rose to Margot's lips.

'Margot is Theatre Sister at the clinic, Mrs Merrick,' Joanne explained calmly, but Eva Merrick was neither impressed nor appeased.

'Such a pity they're not more selective these days about whom they employ,' she remarked scathingly, her cold eyes raking Margot from head to foot once again as if she were some disgusting object which had been placed in her path.

'They are extremely selective, Mrs Merrick,' Joanne contradicted, forestalling Margot once again in a voice that contained a hint of acid. 'People are employed on merit, and not status.'

Eva Merrick's lips thinned into a hard line, but she was not given the opportunity to say more as Joanne swung Margot away from her.

'Sorry about that,' Joanne muttered apologetically, then she added with a spurt of anger, 'That woman needs to be knocked off her high and mighty pedestal, and I hope I'm there one day to see it happen!'

Margot silently echoed Joanne's sentiments, but she very much doubted whether anyone would ever succeed in bringing Eva Merrick down a peg or two.

Moments later a strong-fingered hand clasped Margot's arm, and she was drawn away from Joanne's side.

'You must forgive my mother her idiosyncrasies, Sister Huntley,' Jordan remarked apologetically. 'I'm afraid she'll never change.'

Margot glanced up at him and smiled a little cynically. 'Don't let it concern you, Dr Merrick, and don't imagine that she's the only one who feels that way about people who live on the other side of the tracks.'

'It seems that Willowmead is still the same in many aspects,' he remarked reflectively.

'You should know, Dr Merrick,' she replied coldly, disengaging her arm from his firm clasp and turning from him just as Joanne announced that dinner was to be served.

Seated opposite Jordan, Margot found herself incapable of doing justice to the superb meal Joanne had prepared. Whenever Margot raised her eyes, it was to find Jordan's narrowed, disturbing glance resting on her, while his mother, seated a little to his right, somehow still managed to indicate her disapproval despite the joviality that existed among the rest of the guests.

Margot could not, in truth, say that she felt out of place. No one, except Eva Merrick, tried to convey to her that she was out of her depth, and Margot soon transgressed beyond the stage where this woman's attitude could hurt her in any way. She was relieved, however, when the meal came to an end and they could all return to the living-room where it would not be necessary for her to sit facing Jordan and his mother. Dr

Grant filled up everyone's glasses, then the conversation died down as he raised a commanding hand for silence.

'Friends, colleagues, I would like you to drink a toast to Dr Jordan Merrick,' Dr Grant said in his deep, gravelly voice, turning towards the new Senior Surgeon, and smiling affably. 'I abhor lengthy speeches, Jordan, so may I just express the hope that your stay in Willowmead—and most especially the clinic—will be long and fruitful in every way, and I also speak for our Senior Director, Dr Ellis, when I say that we are extremely fortunate in having a man of your experience as a colleague.' He raised his glass amidst the murmur of voices echoing his wishes. 'Shall we drink to that?'

Glasses were raised in order to drink a toast to the guest of honour, then Jordan himself rose to his feet, his tall, imposing frame commanding everyone's attention. He glanced about the room, then a humorous expression flitted across his face as he said: 'I presume it's expected of me to reply to that?'

'We'll be disappointed if you don't,' Dr Neil Harris chipped in at once, and a burst of goodnatured laughter followed.

'It's good to be on familiar soil once more,' Jordan announced when he had everyone's attention once more, 'and I shall stay as long as the clinic keeps up its reputation for employing the prettiest and most efficient nurses.' Amidst the titter of laughter his dark glance rested momentarily on Margot, and a wave of embarrassed colour surged into her cheeks before he shifted his glance in the direction of the buxom woman seated at the other end of the room. He raised his glass in salute, and smiled faintly. 'May I propose, then, that we drink a toast to Matron Selby and the girls under her command.'

Matron Selby's bosom seemed to expand beneath the jersey cloth bodice of her dress, and Margot felt Joanne nudging her lightly in the ribs to capture her attention before whispering, 'If Matron's not careful she'll snap her stays!'

Margot swallowed her laughter down with a mouthful of wine and very nearly choked, then Joanne took her arm and drew her from the room.

'Come on, Margot,' she said. 'Let's bring in the coffee and try to sober everyone up.'

The evening progressed without further incident, although Margot and Eva Merrick pointedly stayed out of each other's way, but Margot was constantly aware of the cold disdain in the elderly woman's eyes whenever they rested on her. She was aware, too, of Jordan's silent appraisal from time to time. It disturbed her, but she managed to shrug it off successfully until a quick glance at the clock on the mantelshelf made her realise that it was time to leave.

'Joanne, it's been a lovely evening, and thank you for inviting me,' she said as Joanne accompanied her into the hall and helped her into her coat.

'I hope we'll see you again, Margot,' Joanne smiled warmly, 'and bring your mother along next time.'

If anyone else had said that, Margot might have become suspicious, but Joanne Grant radiated a calm sincerity that was unmistakable, and Margot heard herself say, 'Thank you, I'll do that.'

'Are you leaving, Sister Huntley?' a deep voice enquired behind them, and Margot swung round to find herself looking a long way up into those dark, disturbing eyes she had tried to avoid all evening.

'I am, Dr Merrick,' she replied stiffly, deciding to ignore him as she turned once more towards Joanne to say, 'Goodnight, and thank you once again.'

'I'll see you home,' Jordan remarked unexpectedly, forcing her to acknowledge his presence as he followed her from the house.

'I have my car here, thank you,' she informed him coldly, but, to her dismay, he followed her out to where she had parked her Mini. 'Dr Merrick,' she began protestingly, fumbling with a shaky hand in her evening purse for her keys, 'there's really no need for you to——'

'I don't like the idea of women driving around alone after dark,' he interrupted forcefully.

'But that's preposterous!' she argued. 'I'm quite capable of looking after myself.'

'I'll follow you in my car all the same, just to make sure that you arrive home safely,' he insisted undauntedly, taking her keys from her cold fingers and unlocking the door on the driver's side for her.

'But, Dr Merrick——'

'Get in,' he ordered abruptly, taking her by the shoulders and almost thrusting her into the car.

She sat there staring up at his tall, broadshouldered frame silhouetted against the night sky while she tried to make up her mind whether to feel annoyed, or flattered that he should be so ridiculously concerned for her safety, but before she could decide one way or the other, her keys were dropped into her lap and the door at her side was firmly closed. She saw him striding towards his car, and recognised it at once as the car which had followed her home two evenings ago. Flattery no longer played a part in her feelings at that moment; only annoyance.

Her fingers fumbled the key into the ignition and moments later the protesting engine coughed into motion. She pulled away with a jerk, her foot heavy on the accelerator, but the headlights of the white Mercedes followed close behind, and she knew that it would be futile to try to lose him on the way.

Jordan's car sat behind her all the way through the quiet streets, and she wondered suddenly whether his stuck-up mother was aware of what he was up to. She giggled when she imagined Eva Merrick's prune-faced disapproval, but the laughter died within her when her Mini bumped over the railway bridge. Jordan followed at a close but safe distance, the headlights of his Mercedes illuminating the interior of her car like two probing eyes observing her every move, and the thought set her teeth on edge.

Margot expected Jordan to drive on once she had driven through her gates, but when she had garaged the Mini she found his Mercedes parked conspicuously outside the house. He stepped from his car as she rounded the house to enter through the front door, but she was bristling with anger when she stood on the small verandah and watched him push open the wooden gate to walk up the uneven path towards her.

'You followed me home from the clinic the other evening,' she accused, swinging into the attack when she felt her pulses react wildly to his presence. 'Why?' she demanded.

'Same reason I followed you now,' he replied, but his easy manner made her explode with angry sarcasm.

'Such concern for someone who lives on the other side of town is quite unnecessary, and totally unconvincing, Dr Merrick, and the sooner you take yourself and your Mercedes back to where you belong, the better for both of us!'

With the street light behind him it was impossible for

her to read his expression, but there was no mistaking the anger in the hands that gripped her arms and jerked her up against him. The unexpected contact with his muscled body rendered her temporarily speechless, then a current of awareness surged through her, and it activated every nerve she possessed until they were vibrantly alive to the virile masculinity he exuded.

'For the second time this evening I sense that I'm being accused of something, though heaven only knows what,' he remarked with an underlying harshness in his voice that made her flinch inwardly. 'But let me tell you something, Margot Huntley. You've become an inverted snob since the days you ran around barefoot with your pigtails flying, and that places you a close second in the category to which my mother belongs!'

His breath was tantalisingly warm against her mouth, and for one palpitating moment she thought that he was going to kiss her, then he thrust her from him unceremoniously with an abrupt 'Goodnight', and strode down the path towards the gate. He slammed it shut behind him, and seconds later she saw the tail-lights of his car disappearing down the dusty street.

Margot was shaking uncontrollably when she finally let herself into the house and locked the door behind her, but she did not want to stop to analyse what had occurred, neither did she want to recall how close she had come to actually wanting a man's kiss.

'Is that you, Margot?' her mother queried from her darkened bedroom.

'Yes, Mum,' Margot replied softly, pausing in the doorway and peering into the darkness with a measure of surprise that her mother should still be awake at such a late hour.

'I thought I heard a car drive away.'

'That was Dr Merrick,' Margot informed her, her pulse quickening even at the mention of his name. 'He insisted on making sure I arrived home safely.'

'That was nice of him.'

'Yes, wasn't it?' Margot replied with faint sarcasm.

'How was your evening?' her mother asked after a slight, almost reflective pause.

'Very pleasant, thanks to Joanne.'

'I'm so glad,' Beryl Huntley sighed. 'Goodnight, dear. Sleep well.'

'Goodnight, Mum.'

Margot crossed the passage to her own room and, discarding her coat, she sat down on her bed without switching on the light. The springs creaked beneath her with a familiarity that went unnoticed as she unwillingly pondered what had transpired between Jordan and herself a few minutes ago. He had forgotten, obviously, his cutting remark eight years ago, but she had remembered every single word as if it had been branded on her memory. He had labelled her an inverted snob this evening, and perhaps that was exactly what she had become as a form of self-defence and self-preservation, but he had omitted to include himself in the category he had placed his mother.

He was despicable, and he had no business to force his unwanted presence on to her, she decided eventually, and, with that thought, she undressed quietly in the darkness and went to bed.

Jordan treated Margot with cold indifference during the days that followed the dinner party at the Chief Surgeon's home, but it suited her that their association should be kept on a strictly clinical level. As it was, she found him far too disturbing most of the time, and the less she had to do with him, the better for her own peace of mind, she thought vexedly.

'I'd like to alter tomorrow's operating schedule,' Jordan announced late one afternoon as he followed Margot into her small office after they had spent a few gruelling hours in the theatre. 'Mrs Kearney's operation will be a lengthy one, so I'd like to do her in the morning, and Mr van Staaden will then be done in the afternoon.'

'Mr van Staaden is Dr Grant's patient,' she reminded him, but she regretted it the next instant when his dark eyes raked her furiously from head to foot.

'I'm well aware of the fact that I'm not the only surgeon in this establishment, Sister Huntley,' he stated harshly, raising himself to his full autocratic height. 'Dr Grant and I have discussed this matter, and it carries his approval, but you don't have to take my word for it, of course.'

She coloured guiltily as he gestured angrily towards the telephone on her desk, indicating that she was free to seek confirmation from Dr Grant, but she shook her head and lowered her eyes beneath the force of his gaze.

'I'm sorry,' she murmured huskily. 'I had no right to question your instructions.'

A stony silence followed her apology, and she shifted her weight uncomfortably from one foot to the other, clasping her trembling hands respectfully behind her back like a first-year nurse awaiting the wrath of a senior personage, then his voice sliced coldly through the antagonistic atmosphere in the office.

'I would appreciate it if you would notify the ward Sisters of the change in tomorrow's schedule,' he said in precise, clipped tones, and she reacted automatically to his authoritative manner.

'I'll do so at once, Dr Merrick.'

The polished leather of his expensive shoes moved beyond her line of vision, and the tension uncoiled within her as she stood there listening to his firm steps growing fainter as he strode down the passage. A sigh escaped her, then she turned towards the telephone on her desk and lifted the receiver off its cradle.

She was reliving that incident in her office when she drove herself home that afternoon, but, from force of habit, she took the turns slowly on the winding road down to the village. On one such turn she stepped on to the brake and, to her horror, nothing happened. The Mini continued on its way, increasing its speed, but she manoeuvred the bend successfully and, somehow, had the presence of mind to change gratingly down into a lower gear. The speed at which she was travelling was considerably reduced, but there was a sharp bend ahead of her, and she knew with terrifying certainty that she would not make it if she did not manage to reduce speed at once. She pulled frantically at the handbrake, and the Mini jerked, slowing sufficiently for her to take the bend successfully, but it did not halt her progress down the mountain. The engine was protesting loudly, and it was at this point that she knew she had to stop the car somehow. There was only one course open for her to take and, heart pounding in her mouth, she swung the steering wheel sharply towards the left, ramming the nose of her car into the wall of rock which had been blasted away originally to build the road.

Her safety belt prevented her from being thrown against the steering wheel on impact, but she flinched visibly at the sound of crunching metal and splintering glass. A white Mercedes flashed passed her at that moment to stop with a squeal of brakes a few metres ahead of her, and seconds later the door at her side was wrenched open to let in a waft of icy air.

'Are you all right?' Jordan Merrick demanded sharply, his trained eyes searching systematically for cuts or bruises, and finding none.

'Yes, I think so,' she grimaced, wishing that her heart would cease its frantic pounding. 'But I don't suppose I can say the same for my car,' she added ruefully.

His keen glance searched her pale face. 'What happened?'

'The brakes failed,' she answered simply.

'My God!' he exploded, looking grim as he undid the belt which held her pinned to her seat, and she was never certain afterwards whether it was shock, the cold mountain air, or his nearness that made her tremble like a leaf as he helped her out of the battered Mini and into the luxurious warmth of his Mercedes.

Margot sat stiffly beside him, not quite knowing what to say as he drove swiftly but skilfully down the remainder of the winding road. They had not exactly been on the best of terms since the party at the Grant home, and neither had that afternoon's altercation helped to alleviate the tense situation. She would have been less surprised, she decided, had he driven past and left her to her own devices, but instead she found herself alone with him in the confined intimacy of his expensive car, and wondering why he should show her the slightest consideration under the circumstances.

'In circumstances such as these, personal feelings are of no consequence,' Jordan remarked as if he had read her thoughts and, at her startled gasp, he shot a swift, mocking glance in her direction. 'I know you dislike me for some reason, Sister Huntley, but it would have been most ungallant of me to have left you stranded along the road at this late hour of the day.'

'I appreciate your help, Dr Merrick, but you're mistaken in thinking that I dislike you,' she told him stiffly but politely.

'Am I?' he smiled cynically without taking his eyes off the road. 'You certainly left me with the distinct impression that you despised me, and all I stood for.'

Margot shifted uncomfortably in her seat. 'I know my place, Dr Merrick.'

'Meaning I don't know mine?' he returned sharply, and when she did not reply, he said wryly, 'Perhaps it would be advisable if we stepped off this particular subject.'

'Perhaps it would,' she agreed readily.

'Do you possess any other form of transport?'

'I have an understanding with the garage manager,' she replied, relieved to be discussing a less personal topic. 'They always provide me with a car while mine is in for repairs.'

Fifteen minutes later arrangements had been made to collect Margot's Mini. There was no vehicle available for her to use at that moment, but she was assured that a car would be delivered to her home early the following morning, and once again Margot found herself seated in Jordan's Mercedes with no option but to accept his offer of a lift to her home.

Why he should go to such lengths to help her, she had no idea, but she was determined not to be trapped once again into thinking him any different from his mother.

'Thank you very much for your assistance, Dr Merrick,' she said hurriedly when she climbed out of his car, but, to her dismay, he followed her example and walked round the bonnet of his car to join her on the pavement at her front gate.

'You could invite me in for something to drink,' he suggested with a hint of reprisal in his voice, but instead of guilt, she experienced a wave of cynical anger flowing through her.

'You're on the wrong side of the tracks, remember.'

'So I am,' he remarked absently, his eyes narrowing in something close to anger. 'I'll come in for a cup of coffee all the same.'

Margot's heart leapt uncomfortably. 'Dr Merrick, I appreciate your kindness, but——'

'Are you ashamed of your home?' he challenged abruptly, and her grey eyes flashed angrily up into his.

'No, of course I'm not!' she exclaimed indignantly. 'But I——'

'Then let's waste no more time standing out here in the cold,' he cut in suavely, taking her arm in a firm grip and almost pushing her through the small wooden gate and up the short path to the front door.

They found her mother in the kitchen busily preparing dinner, and Margot temporarily forgot her annoyance with Jordan when her mother turned to confront them. Beryl Huntley was only just in her fifties, but at that moment she looked years older, and Margot's throat tightened painfully as she went up to her mother and kissed her affectionately on her flushed cheek.

'Mum, you remember Dr Merrick, don't you?' Margot asked, indicating the man who stood observing them from across the room with a faint smile curving his lips.

'Yes, of course,' her mother replied at once, her thin features creasing into a smile of recognition as Jordan stepped forward to take her thin hand in his. 'You gave me a lift home in the rain once, but that was years ago when you were still a student, Dr Merrick,' Beryl reminded him.

'The name's Jordan, Mrs Huntley,' he smiled down at the older woman with a warmth Margot had not noticed before. 'I remember the incident very well,' he assured her, then he asked with something more than politeness, 'How are you?'

'Oh ...' Beryl Huntley gestured laughingly, 'getting older, as you can see.'

'You don't look a day older than the last time I saw you,' Jordan assured her gallantly but untruthfully, and to Margot's surprise her mother seemed to shed several years beneath his flattering attention. 'I was hoping we would meet again,' he added convincingly.

'I was hoping the same when I heard that you'd returned to Willowmead,' Beryl replied at once, tilting her head up at him with a warm questioning smile flitting across her features. 'Will you stay for a cup of coffee?'

'I was hoping you would ask, Mrs Huntley,' Jordan admitted, slanting a mocking glance in Margot's direction which made her stiffen in silent protest while she removed her cape and unpinned her starched cap.

'You're home late this afternoon, Margot,' her mother remarked when they sat around the scrubbed kitchen table drinking their coffee.

Margot shot a warning glance in Jordan's direction as she said carefully, 'I ... had trouble with my car along the way, and Dr Merrick kindly offered me a lift home.'

'That was very kind of you, Jordan,' her mother smiled across the table at him. 'I always worry about her when she's driving around in that car of hers, and it hasn't been in such good shape lately.'

'There's nothing wrong with my car that can't be

fixed, Mum,' Margot protested instantly, ignoring Jordan's contradictory glance.

'If you say so, dear,' her mother shrugged, returning her attention to their guest.

Jordan's immaculate presence in their small, homely kitchen disturbed Margot, but he appeared to be completely at ease, his long legs stretched out comfortably beneath the table, and a smile playing about his chiselled mouth while he listened attentively to something her mother was saying.

'It looks so damned right that he should be sitting there,' she thought suspiciously. 'But what's he trying to prove?'

Her glance dwelled searchingly on his features, on the dark hair brushed back so severely from his broad forehead, the heavy eyebrows, the aristocratic nose, and the strong, square jaw beneath the faintly sensuous mouth. His complexion was tanned as if he had spent long hours in the sun, and there clung to him an aura of virile masculinity which she had found impossible to ignore. His eyes burned into hers unexpectedly and, despite her years of strenuous training as a nurse, she could not prevent the guilty flush from surging up into her cheeks. Her heart began to pound at an alarming rate, and she looked away hurriedly, furious with herself for being caught staring.

'Your mother doesn't look well,' Jordan remarked when she eventually accompanied him out to his car.

'I know,' she agreed stiffly, 'but that's my problem, and not yours.'

His eyebrows rose sharply as he paused at the gate to look down at her. 'Do you object to my interest in your mother's health?'

'I fail to see why it should interest you,' she replied defensively.

'That doesn't surprise me,' he remarked caustically. 'If you ask me, there are many things you fail to see while you're so busy burying yourself behind that wall of prejudice you've erected about yourself.'

Her small chin rose defiantly, and flint sharp anger sparked in her eyes. 'When I want your opinion, I'll ask for it, Dr Merrick.'

'I doubt it,' he stated abruptly, a wry smile curving his mouth. 'Thank your mother for the coffee. Her hospitality was commendable.'

'While mine was not, I gather,' she snapped, but she could have bitten off her tongue the next moment when the street light illuminated the gleam of mockery in his dark eyes.

'You said it, Sister Huntley, not I,' he told her blandly, and Margot was fuming inwardly moments later as she watched him drive away down the street.

Jordan had won this round with ease, and she had a sinking feeling that it would always be so.

# CHAPTER THREE

IT was a few days after smashing her Mini into the side of the mountain that Margot lingered over a cup of tea during her lunch hour and allowed her thoughts the privilege of dwelling on Jordan Merrick. It seemed to her that the operating theatre was the only place where they could spend time together without friction causing the sparks to fly. They worked together like a well-rehearsed team, and in complete harmony with each other. Margot's professional admiration and respect for him as a surgeon had increased swiftly since that first day they had worked together in the theatre, but her personal feelings were still in a turmoil, and it was best not to unravel them, she decided uneasily.

'May I join you?'

Margot looked up sharply to find the object of her thoughts standing beside her favourite table in the corner of the canteen, and her heart leapt uncomfortably in her breast. He was too damned good-looking, she decided as she met his glance with unwavering grey eyes and said coldly, 'If you must, Dr Merrick.'

His chiselled mouth twisted into a semblance of a smile as he placed his cup of tea on the table and pulled out a chair to seat himself opposite her.

'Tell me, Sister Huntley, are you always this unsociable, or do you reserve that side of your nature exclusively for someone like myself?'

Margot's hands tightened in her lap. 'Let's just say

that I prefer my own company at times.'

'And this is one of those times, I take it.'

'That's right,' she snapped, antagonism rising sharply within her.

She drank her tea hurriedly now, trying to ignore his presence at her table, but she found it virtually impossible not to be aware of the magnetism he somehow exuded.

'I believe they serve an excellent meal at that new motel just out of town,' he was saying, and when she looked up questioningly he added: 'Have dinner there with me this evening?'

Surprise rendered her momentarily speechless, then she shook her head decisively. 'I'm sorry, but it's out of the question.'

'Why?' he shot the question at her, his dark eyes probing disturbingly beneath her cool exterior.

'Does there have to be a reason?' she asked evasively.

'There usually is when a woman turns down a man's invitation,' he insisted mockingly, and it was his mockery that lit the fire of her anger.

'A woman has the right to choose whom she does or does not wish to go out with, and I choose not to have dinner with you.'

'What are you afraid of?' he demanded quietly, leaning towards her across the table and gripping her wrist with those strong, lean fingers. 'Are you afraid of me . . . or yourself?'

'Neither,' she snapped, and as her pulse quickened beneath his touch, she wrenched her hand from his and pushed back her chair. 'Excuse me, Dr Merrick, I have work to do.'

His tall, broad-shouldered frame barred her way instantly, and she drew back in alarm when her nerves vibrated at his nearness.

'I'll call for you at seven,' he told her with annoying persistence.

'I shan't be dining with you, Dr Merrick,' she assured him coldly, but his arrogantly mocking smile did not waver for an instant.

'We'll see about that.'

He stood aside for her to pass and, seething inwardly, Margot marched out of the canteen and into the warm winter sunshine. 'We'll see about that!' she echoed his words furiously. 'We shall see whether I have dinner with you this evening or not!'

Margot assisted Dr Grant in the theatre that afternoon and, as a result, she did not see Jordan again. The hours in the theatre had been long and tiring, sweeping all personal thoughts from her mind, and it was almost six o'clock that evening when she arrived at her home.

'Shall I put on the dinner for you, Mum?' she asked, noticing the absence of the cooking pots on the stove.

'No, dear,' her mother shook her head firmly. 'You get yourself ready for your dinner date with Jordan.'

'My *what*?' Margot demanded incredulously.

'You heard me,' her mother smiled tolerantly. 'Now hurry up, dear. You haven't much time, you know.'

'Mum, will you please explain what's going on?' Margot demanded, puzzled as to how her mother had heard of Jordan's invitation, but the answer, when it came, was so logical that she could have kicked herself for not having thought of it herself.

'Jordan came round early this afternoon to ask if I would object to you dining out with him this evening and, naturally, I said I had no objection to it at all.'

'Did he also mention that I'd refused his invitation?' Margot asked, finding difficulty in suppressing her anger as she faced her mother.

'We talked for such a long time, I really can't remember whether he mentioned it or not,' her mother replied, looking a little vague, then she pulled herself together and gestured impatiently. 'Go on, now. Get yourself ready.'

'I shall do nothing of the kind,' Margot protested, facing her mother squarely. 'I'm not going to have dinner with him. Not this evening. Not *ever*!'

Disappointment washed over Beryl's tired features. 'Oh, but I said you would, and he's already made the necessary arrangements. You can't back out now, Margot.'

'Oh, Mum!' she sighed exasperatedly.

'Couldn't you go even if it's just to please me, dear?'

Against her will, Margot relented, and an hour later she re-entered the kitchen to find Jordan involved in what appeared to be a serious discussion with her mother. Did she imagine it, Margot wondered afterwards, or did her mother flash a warning glance at Jordan when she looked up to see her entering the kitchen?

'You look lovely, dear,' her mother smiled happily. 'Doesn't she look lovely, Jordan?'

'Lovely,' Jordan agreed, rising to his feet and sliding his dark glance over Margot's slender, feminine curves beneath the cinnamon-coloured silk of her evening dress. Her breath stilled in her throat as she experienced the peculiar sensation that she had been caressed, then he broke the spell he had woven about her by saying, 'Shall we go?'

'If you like,' Margot replied, turning towards her mother to hide the flush that stained her cheeks. 'Will you be all right, Mum?'

'Of course, dear,' her mother insisted, getting up to kiss Margot's cheek lightly. 'Enjoy yourselves.'

'That was a foul thing to do!' Margot accused Jordan the moment they were alone and speeding away in his Mercedes. 'How dared you go to my mother behind my back when I'd already made it clear to you that I had no wish to accept your invitation?'

'You didn't have to agree,' he reminded her with that infuriating calmness which seemed to raise her blood pressure by several degrees.

'No, I didn't have to agree,' she admitted furiously, 'but you knew I'd do anything not to upset my mother, didn't you?'

The light of the dashboard intensified every harsh, mocking line of his features as he glanced at her briefly. 'Let's say that I took a gamble, and it paid off.'

'I think you're despicable!' she retorted, caught up in a wave of helpless anger.

'I don't know what you have against me,' he laughed unexpectedly, 'but I have a feeling that we could enjoy each other's company if only you'd relax a little.'

'If ever I were in need of company, you'd be the last person I would turn to,' she assured him heatedly.

'That's not very complimentary.'

'It was not intended as a compliment,' she snapped at him.

'I can see we're going to spend an exciting evening together,' he observed with a derisive note in his voice.

'I certainly hope you enjoy yourself,' she replied scathingly, but her reply merely evoked his mocking laughter.

'Oh, I shall enjoy myself, believe me.'

A tense silence settled between them as they left the village behind them and sped towards the motel.

Margot was fuming inwardly, but Jordan seemed unperturbed by her obvious reluctance to spend the evening in his company, and later, throughout the superb meal he had ordered, he made several unsuccessful attempts to draw her out of her angry shell.

'You hardly touched your food,' he remarked when she refused a second glass of wine.

'I'm not very hungry.'

'You're determined not to enjoy the evening, it seems,' he observed dryly.

'Did you imagine I would?' she demanded sarcastically.

'You puzzle me, Margot,' he remarked at length, and her name sounded strangely musical on his lips. 'I can't quite make up my mind whether you don't like men generally, or whether you don't like me in particular.' His eyes, dark and probing, met hers across the candle-lit table. 'Have I ever done anything to deserve your dislike?'

'Yes, you did do something!' she wanted to cry out, but she bit back the words and said instead, 'You could answer that question better than I can.'

'I can't for the life of me think of anything I may have done,' he stated frowningly, then his eyes roamed over her with a searching intensity that sent a now familiar warmth stealing into her cheeks. 'You've changed, Margot. I seem to remember a girl with pigtails, freckles, and laughing grey eyes.'

'That was a long time ago,' she reminded him, swallowing nervously now as she lowered her lashes to avoid his intense scrutiny. 'I outgrew the pigtail stage, and there's seldom anything to laugh about these days.'

'There's still a dusting of freckles on your nose, I notice.'

Embarrassed, she changed the subject. 'I believe you didn't come home to Willowmead during your last year at varsity.'

'That's so,' he acknowledged thoughtfully. 'You could say that my mother and I had a difference of opinion, and by mutual consent I spent my holidays elsewhere. After that I won a scholarship to study in Europe, and I remained there for seven years.'

'What made you decide to come back after all this time?' she heard herself ask.

'Would you believe homesickness?' He saw the mocking disbelief in her eyes, and laughed shortly. 'No, I thought you wouldn't.'

'Why would homesickness bring you back to South Africa when your father's death failed to do so two years ago?'

'Circumstances prevented me from flying out to attend the funeral.'

'Were those circumstances feminine and pretty?' she mocked him openly, and his tight-lipped expression told her that she had scored a hit.

'Pretty isn't quite the right adjective I would have used to describe Helga,' he surprised Margot with his reply. 'She was one of the most beautiful women I'd ever seen, and added to that she was an outstanding pathologist.'

'Was?' Margot queried, finding it curious that he should speak of this woman in the past tense.

'She's dead.'

That flat, harsh statement sent a shock of mixed emotions rippling through Margot. Dismay, regret and compassion clamoured for supremacy, but there was something else, too; something which she hesitated to define.

'I'm sorry,' she said lamely, but the words seemed so inadequate to explain what she was feeling at that moment and, as if to make him aware of this, her hand reached out impulsively across the table to clasp his. 'I really *am* sorry,' she assured him.

To touch him like that sent a quivering sensation along her nerves which intensified when his fingers tightened briefly about hers before he allowed her to draw her hand away, and then it was Jordan who changed the subject.

'What made you decide to take up nursing as a career?'

'It was the next best thing to studying medicine,' she replied with a candidness she would have avoided earlier in the evening, and she smiled faintly when his heavy eyebrows rose in surprise.

'You never told me you were interested in becoming a doctor.'

'You never asked,' she answered wryly, 'and at that time I didn't exactly know you well enough to confide in you.'

His glance sharpened. 'Do you have any regrets about not being able to study further?'

'Sometimes, yes, but being a nurse is a very rewarding and gratifying job. Besides, I . . .' She paused, smiling at the memory of her intense misery all those years ago when she had failed in her application for a bursary, but she thrust aside the memory now as she became aware of Jordan observing her intently. 'I'm not the type to become neurotic about the things I know I can't have,' she added convincingly, but she did not succeed entirely in hiding the hint of sadness in her voice.

For the first time since meeting Jordan again, Margot

found herself relaxing and feeling oddly at ease with him. In the car, later that evening, she leaned back in her seat and closed her eyes for a moment, but her uneasiness returned with lightning swiftness when he parked the car on a rise just outside Willowmead.

'Why are you stopping?' she asked, sitting up abruptly and turning her eyes from the lights of the village below them to glance at him warily.

'Where else can we talk privately without people staring at us curiously?' he asked, turning towards her and sliding an arm along the back of the seat behind her shoulders.

'What is there we have to discuss that needs such privacy?' she demanded, cautiously edging a little away from him when his nearness filled her nostrils with the clean, tantalising male scent of him.

'I'll think of something,' he mocked her, capturing one of her hands in his.

'Please ... it's late, and ...' His warm lips brushed against the inside of her wrist where her pulse was beating at an erratic pace, and small, electrifying tremors began to shoot up her arm before spreading throughout her entire body. 'Don't do that!' she begged in a soft, frantic voice.

'Why not?' he demanded, raising his dark head so that her bewildered eyes fastened themselves on to his strong features etched so clearly in the moonlight.

'Don't—don't spoil the evening,' she begged haltingly.

His mouth curved in a suspicion of a smile. 'You have enjoyed it, then?'

'Yes, I have,' she admitted truthfully, adding to his triumph while she carefully removed her hand from his clasp.

'Will you have dinner with me again some time soon?'

'Perhaps,' she prevaricated.

'Don't be evasive,' he commanded roughly. 'Give me a straight "yes" or "no".'

'No!' Her mind screamed out the answer, but the word that passed her lips was a breathless, 'Yes.'

Her fluttering hand was captured and held against his chest where she could feel the hard warmth of his body through the thin silk of his white shirt. Never before had she been so aware of him as a man, and never had she been made so conscious of her own vulnerable femininity. She tried to draw away from him, but a terrifying weakness had somehow invaded her limbs.

'You're trembling,' Jordan observed, his voice deepening to a sensual caress that made the blood leap through her veins.

'I—I'm cold,' she lied in desperation.

'That's easily remedied,' he said at once, and reaching across into the back of the car he produced a small travelling rug which he draped about her with care.

He was so close to her now that she could feel the heat of his body against her own. She knew instinctively what was about to happen, but, even as her mind sent out frantic warning signals, she stilled beneath his touch as his fingers roamed lightly through her hair. His warm breath mingled with hers as his hand tightened at the nape of her neck, then his mouth took possession of hers in a light, exploratory kiss that stirred her senses into a wild crescendo and, without realising what she was doing, she moved closer to him, her lips parting voluntarily beneath his as his kiss deepened and lengthened into something that drove every vestige of thought from her mind.

She was in a dazed and bemused state when he finally raised his head, but sanity returned painfully when she stared up into his face just above hers. She tried to draw away from him, but his arms tightened about her, and his name was a low moan on her lips before he crushed them beneath his own in a searingly passionate kiss that lit an answering flame within her. His hands were beneath her coat, moving with intoxicating slowness over her body until they cupped her breasts through the fine silk of her dress. No one had ever touched her with such intimacy before, but the natural instinct to withdraw was swept aside by the rising tide of emotions she had not thought she possessed, and it left her powerless to do anything other than cling to him while every nerve and sinew in her body seemed to come alive to his touch.

His lips trailed across her flushed cheek and found a sensitive spot behind her ear. A shiver of delight rippled through her, then his lips went on to explore her slender, exposed throat where a pulse throbbed in wild response to his touch, and then he once more found her eager lips with his own. Margot had never dreamed that anything could be this exquisite and, with the moon and the stars as her only witnesses, she lost herself completely in the magic of the moment. Jordan's snide remark, made so many years ago, was no longer of any importance. She had, in fact, not even given it a thought, but it all returned with stunning swiftness to taunt her, and fill her with such intense shame that she wished the earth would open up beneath her when Jordan finally thrust her away from him with an angry exclamation on his lips.

Harsh, hurtful words sprang to her lips, but she choked them back when he started the car and drove her home in silence. His abrupt 'Goodnight' when they parted company did nothing to ease her misery, and she spent a sleepless night cursing herself for her own stupidity. She had been like malleable clay in his experienced hands, succumbing to his kisses, and responding with a fervour she knew she would be ashamed of for the rest of her life.

'It's that kid from the other side of town, and it surprises me, Mother, that you haven't yet told her we have a tradesmen's entrance for people like her.'

Those words, uttered so long ago, returned to haunt her, and she knew, with painful certainty, that Jordan Merrick would never think of her in any other way. She was someone from the other side of town; someone he could play around with for his own amusement, but never with any serious intent.

When the sun started its slow climb into the wintry sky, it found Margot wide awake and nursing a throbbing headache which abated reluctantly after she had been forced to swallow down a couple of aspirins.

'How was your evening out with Jordan?' Beryl Huntley asked inquisitively when Margot peeped into her bedroom before going to work.

'It was all right, I suppose,' Margot brushed aside the question, her clinical glance taking in her mother's pale, drawn features against the pillows. 'Mum, you don't look at all well. Why don't you stay in bed, then I'll give Dr Turner a call and ask him to come round and take a look at you.'

'Nonsense! I'm feeling fine!' her mother protested. 'You go to the clinic, dear. I'll be all right.'

'But I don't like——'

'Margot dear, don't fuss so,' Beryl interrupted her daughter impatiently, and Margot sighed inwardly as she leaned over her mother to kiss her on the cheek.

She went to work that morning with a measure of reluctance. She was more than ordinarily concerned about her mother, and then there was still the problem of having to face Jordan after what had occurred the night before. She need not have concerned herself about the latter, for Jordan's cool, aloof attitude, combined with her years of training, helped her to survive that day, and also the days that followed. Her suspicions about him were finally confirmed when rumours of marriage to the daughter of an eminently successful Cape Town business man did the rounds, and though she told herself that she did not care, she nevertheless suffered an odd little stab in the region of her heart.

A curious desolation seemed to take possession of Margot. Her Mini had been returned to her almost as good as new and, feeling the need to be alone, she drove away from her home the Sunday afternoon and headed towards the river, her favourite stopping place when she needed to sort her muddled thoughts into their proper perspective.

'So *what* if he's planning to be married?' she asked herself irritably some time later when she had got out of her car to sit on the deserted grassy embankment. The water flowed lazily on its way to the ocean, but Margot's thoughts were far removed from the geographical progress of the river as she sat staring blankly at the rippling waters. She seldom paid much attention to the rumours which so often reached her ears at the clinic, and mostly there would be no truth in them, but this particular rumour disturbed her intensely for some inexplicable reason.

It was naturally no concern of hers, and Jordan Merrick was free to do as he pleased. The only thing that concerned her was that he should continue to leave her in peace to live down the shame of the emotions he had aroused in her with such a diabolical cleverness.

A twig snapped behind her, and her heart lurched with a violence that made the earth seem to tilt beneath her as she glanced over her shoulder to fasten her startled gaze on the tall, muscular figure approaching her. In brown suede pants and red ski jacket Jordan looked dangerously tough and relentless, and she scrambled hastily to her feet, her pulses leaping jerkily in all directions when he paused a few paces away from her to sweep her from head to foot with those penetrating dark eyes. She felt, peculiarly, as if those eyes had stripped her naked and, flustered, she bent down to brush the dry grass from her slacks, but her hands were shaking to such an extent that she relinquished the effort and clasped them behind her back instead.

'Good afternoon, Dr Merrick,' she managed with a cool politeness that did not match the turmoil raging within her, and he inclined his dark head in that same distant manner he had used towards her since that evening she had dined with him at the motel. 'I never expected to see you here,' she added, despising herself for the nervous tremor that had crept into her voice.

'Your mother told me where I would find you,' he supplied the answer to her unspoken question as he thrust his hands into the pockets of his pants and lessened the distance between them. He glanced about him briefly, taking in the willow trees stripped bare of their foliage, then his eyes fastened on to hers once more with a strange intensity. 'Do you come here often?'

'When I feel the need to be on my own, yes,' she replied without hesitation, hoping that he would take that as a hint to leave her alone, but when he made no move to go she realised that he had no intention of granting her her wish.

'About the other night, Margot——' he began, but she waved him to silence with an abrupt gesture of distaste.

'Perhaps it would be a good thing if we just forgot about it.'

His jaw hardened ominously. 'Have you been able to forget what happened?'

'I haven't given it a thought since,' she lied desperately, but her breath caught in her throat when his hands fastened themselves on to her shoulders in a bone-crushing grip.

'Don't lie to me!' he commanded harshly, his eyes burning into hers as if he wanted to strip her to her very soul and, frightened of what he might find there, she lowered her glance to the tanned column of his strong throat where the hair on his chest was clearly visible above the top button of his brown, open-necked shirt.

His hands slid down her arms to encircle her waist, and she was suddenly besieged with the mad desire to know again the touch of his lips. 'Oh, God, help me, please!' she prayed silently and desperately and, closing her eyes to shut out the temptation, she twisted herself free of his hold.

'Why can't you leave me alone?' she cried despairingly after she had moved a safe distance away from him. 'I've written off that incident to experience. Why can't you do the same?'

'Do you think I haven't tried?' he lashed out at her harshly.

'Then try harder!' she almost shouted at him, fighting against the pain which seemed to tear her insides apart.

'Oh, no!' he exclaimed, white about the mouth as he

bridged the gap between them in one long stride and swung her round to face him. 'I didn't come here to argue with you. I thought we could sit down and discuss the situation like two civilised people, but it seems I was mistaken in you.'

'Yes, you *are* mistaken,' she hit back, her eyes flashing blue flames of defensive anger. 'We have absolutely nothing to discuss with each other, and as far as I'm concerned the incident is over and forgotten.'

'Like hell it is!' Jordan ground out the words, lashing his arms about her in a vice-like grip, and imprisoning her against the hard length of his body. 'Like hell it's over and forgotten,' he repeated through clenched teeth, and fear mingled with intolerable excitement in those brief seconds before his mouth descended to devour hers.

Against her will, her taut body relaxed beneath the passionate onslaught of his kisses, and her emotions soared to a level where she was no longer conscious of anything other than his lips and his hands, and the hard pressure of his muscular thighs against her own as he bore her down on to the grass. His hand was beneath her sweater, gripping her waist and moving upward determinedly to caress the sensitive hollow of her back. The catch of her lacy bra gave way beneath his fingers, and a low moan of pleasure burst from her lips when she felt him clasp the soft swell of her breast. His touch was firm, experienced, and her body responded with a pulsating swiftness until the sweet agony of desire brought her to her senses and made her stiffen beneath his hands.

His eyes were dark and stormy with suppressed passion when he raised his head to glance at her enquiringly, and in that moment, as his hold on her relaxed, she rolled away from him and leapt to her feet.

'Leave me alone, Jordan Merrick!' she cried hoarsely, despising herself for being so weak. 'I don't intend that you should use me as a plaything with which to amuse yourself in your idle moments!'

Jordan got to his feet slowly, his expression thunderous as he towered over her. 'What exactly is that supposed to mean?'

'Just what I said,' she repeated, raising her chin defiantly, and praying that he would not see the torment she was experiencing. 'I'm not available for your amusement.'

'I don't recall stating that I was seeking amusement,' he remarked with admirable self-control, and the sudden absence of emotion on his attractively chiselled features merely heightened her fury.

'What else would someone like yourself want on this side of town?'

Margot regretted those words the moment they were spoken. It was not always wise to voice one's opinions, and she was made aware of her error when she glimpsed Jordan's granite-hard expression. His eyes, like coals of fire, scorched her from head to foot, and she shrivelled inwardly with fear and shame.

'Make my apologies to your mother,' his voice grated along her raw, sensitive nerves. 'I shan't be staying for tea.'

Margot watched him through pain-filled eyes as he climbed into his car and drove away, and she shivered suddenly as if he had taken the warmth of the sun with him. She had said too much, perhaps, without considering her choice of words, but it was done, and it was ridiculous to feel as if she had lost something of value.

'Where's Jordan?' Beryl wanted to know when

Margot arrived home to find her setting out a plate of jam tarts for tea.

'He sent his apologies.'

'But why?' her mother wanted to know, her hands stilling as her bewildered glance became fixed intently on Margot's pale cheeks. 'What happened to change his mind?'

Margot looked away uncomfortably and shrugged with affected casualness. 'We had a difference of opinion.'

'Oh, Margot!' Beryl shook her head admonishingly. 'There are times when I think I'll never understand you.'

'There are times when I don't understand myself,' Margot laughed, but her laughter sounded hollow as she turned away swiftly to hide the film of tears in her eyes before escaping to her bedroom.

There was no escape, however, from the memory of those moments in Jordan's arms. She could still feel the touch of his lips and hands, and her treacherous body tingled with the memory of forbidden excitement. She despised herself for allowing her thoughts to linger on the incident, and she cringed with shame when she recalled her own response, but the knowledge that her heart had not escaped unscathed caused her the greatest discomfort and pain of all at that moment.

# CHAPTER FOUR

THE Monday morning started entirely wrong for Margot. First of all the geyser had developed a fault during the night, which meant that Margot had to shiver her way through a tepid bath, then the Mini was reluctant to start on that cold, bleak morning and, as a result, she arrived late at the clinic. One of the theatre nurses went off sick with pneumonia, and for some obscure reason no one had thought to find someone to take her place. When Margot finally managed to find a replacement the scheduled operation had been delayed by several minutes, and Daniel Grant, normally an even-tempered man, was breathing fire at everyone, most especially Margot, for what he considered gross negligence.

Throughout it all Margot's composure never faltered, but she sighed with relief several hours later when the patient was wheeled from the theatre without any further mishaps occurring. She headed wearily towards the wash-room, but a heavy hand on her shoulder detained her, and she turned to find the Chief Surgeon smiling down at her a little crookedly with his theatre mask pulled down to beneath his chin.

'My apologies, Margot,' said Daniel Grant, his fingers tightening briefly on her shoulder before he removed his hand. 'I don't think you deserved the sharp edge of my tongue.'

'I understand, Dr Grant,' she replied hastily, pulling down her own mask to breathe easier. 'The theatre is my department. It's my job to see that things run smoothly, and I was equally annoyed at the delay.'

Always a man of few words, Daniel Grant nodded and strode from the theatre, his theatre boots squeaking on the tiled floor. Margot followed him a few minutes later and ordered tea to be sent to her office in preference to having lunch in the canteen. Jordan was scheduled to operate that afternoon, but she did not want to think of having to face him yet as she pulled her log book closer and brought it up to date.

Two hours later Margot was on duty once more in the theatre and, gowned and masked, she murmured reassurances to the patient who had been wheeled in. Neil Harris, the anaesthetist, winked at Margot across the prostrate figure on the operating table.

'I hope Merrick's in a better mood than the Chief was this morning,' he muttered, and Margot was echoing his wish silently when the doors swung open to admit Jordan.

She did not have to turn around to know that it was him; she felt his presence in every fibre of her being, but it was only when his green-gowned figure took up position beside her that she found the courage to raise her glance to his. His dark eyes appraised her with a cool indifference that made her wince inwardly, and she looked away hastily, trying to control that choking sensation which threatened to fill her eyes with humiliating tears. Jordan indicated to Neil Harris that he was ready to begin and, taking a steadying breath, Margot thrust aside her personal problems to concentrate on the task before her.

The operation could not have been in progress more than fifteen minutes when she became aware of someone moving quietly to her side.

'Sister Huntley,' she recognised Sister Lewis's voice from behind the theatre mask. 'I'll take over from here,' Sister Lewis continued with some urgency. 'Matron would like to see you in her office at once.'

This disturbance did not go unnoticed, and Jordan snapped angrily, 'This is highly irregular!'

'I know, Dr Merrick,' Sister Lewis assured him swiftly, 'but this is an emergency.'

In a hospital an emergency could range from a fire in the wards to a major civil catastrophe, but in a clinic which specialised in plastic surgery for patients who had been considered beyond help, Margot had no idea what could be considered serious enough to necessitate changing Theatre Sisters while an operation was in progress. She did not stop to ponder this, however, and she shed her theatre garments with more speed than usual before hurrying along the passages to Matron Selby's office.

Margot had been there only once before, and that was when she had been interviewed for the position of Theatre Sister, but as she stood outside that panelled door, she experienced again that same tautening of her nerves before she raised her hand and knocked lightly. Matron's booming voice commanded her to enter at once, and Margot stepped into the room to find Daniel Grant there as well. His hands were thrust into his pockets, and his expression was grim as he stood with his back to the window facing the buxom woman seated behind the large, cluttered desk.

'Oh, dear, what have I done?' Margot wondered, fighting down her panic as she clasped her hands respectfully behind her back and moistened her dry lips. Then she said nervously, 'I believe you wanted to see me, Matron.'

Matron Selby's glance darted towards the Chief Surgeon in a curious gesture of appeal, but he merely shook his head as if to say, 'This is your department, Matron', and crossed the room towards the door.

'I'll be in my office if you should need me later,' he announced, then the panelled door closed behind his tall figure, and Margot found herself alone with the woman who was her formidable superior.

'Sister Huntley——' Matron began at length when the silence had stretched to breaking point. 'Your mother was rushed to the general hospital a half hour ago. I think you should go there at once. Dr Turner is waiting for you.'

Those words had been spoken gently, and with obvious difficulty, but they had struck Margot with a force which had made her reel mentally. An eternity seemed to pass while she assimilated the news which had drained every vestige of colour from her face, but it could, in fact, only have been seconds before she regained control of herself to say shakily, 'Thank you, Matron.'

'If you need any help——' Matron halted Margot's hasty departure, but Margot shook her head decisively.

'I'll manage, thank you,' she muttered, and less than five minutes later she was driving towards the general hospital with as much speed as she could cope with while keeping within the margin of safety. The Mini's engine protested loudly to the unaccustomed weight of her foot on the accelerator, but she was deaf to everything except the loud drumming of fear in her ears.

Dr Turner met her at the Casualty entrance and as he led her down a short passage beyond the admittance office, she asked anxiously, 'What happened? What's wrong with my mother?'

'Come in here, and sit down,' he said, ushering her

into an empty waiting-room and indicating towards a chair, but she shook her head impatiently and remained standing.

'Where is she? Can I see her?'

Dr Turner, a kindly man in his fifties, shook his head and said quietly, 'She's in the operating theatre. I had to call in the services of Dr Russell, and he decided on an immediate operation.'

'Operation?' Margot repeated confusedly. 'But I——'

'Sit down, Margot,' he instructed, pushing her gently into a chair and seating himself opposite her. 'For a long time now I've been treating your mother for a tumour in the stomach. I've suggested before that she come in for tests and a possible operation, but she's been putting it off.' Margot's expression must have conveyed her complete bewilderment, and his bushy eyebrows rose sharply. 'You didn't know about this?'

Margot shivered despite the warmth of the air-conditioned room. 'I knew she was seeing you at regular intervals, but she led me to believe it was a slight digestive problem coupled with anaemia.'

'Damn!' Dr Turner muttered, his mouth tightening.

The professional side of Margot's brain started functioning once more, and her years of training in the general wards made her ask, 'Was she haemorrhaging when she was brought in this afternoon?'

'I'm afraid so,' Dr Turner replied, fishing in his pockets for a cigarette, but discarding the idea moments later.

'What are her chances?' she asked, her glance unwavering as she waited with bated breath for him to speak.

A humourless smile curved the doctor's mouth. 'What you really want to know is whether I think the tumour is cancerous or not, and that I can't say until the necessary tests have been done.' His expression sobered to one of severity and concern. 'At the moment we must trouble ourselves only with the problem of whether or not your mother is strong enough to survive the operation. She's lost a tremendous amount of blood,' he added unnecessarily just as his name was announced over the intercom system stating that he was needed in Casualty. He rose at once and gripped her shoulder briefly. 'I have to leave you now, Margot, but I'll have them send in a cup of strong tea. You look as though you could use one.'

Alone in the waiting-room, Margot paced the floor restlessly. The tea arrived and she drank it almost without thinking to continue her pacing. Her experience in the theatre of this very hospital brought to mind so many things that could go wrong when a patient such as her mother was wheeled in for surgery, and fear raced chillingly through her veins as every re-membered incident flashed before her eyes, like a film on a screen.

The tension within her had become almost unbear-able when a familiar, soothing voice spoke her name, and she swung round to see Joanne Grant entering the waiting room.

'Daniel telephoned,' she explained briefly, taking Margot's cold hands in her own and gripping them with a comforting warmth. 'How is your mother?'

'I don't know yet,' Margot replied, trying to smile, but her lips refused to obey. 'She's still in the theatre.'

'How bad is it?'

'If she survives the operation there's still a possibility that the tumour might be cancerous, and if that's con-firmed, then——'

'Don't, my dear,' Joanne interrupted, her green eyes conveying sympathetic understanding as her warm hands tightened about Margot's cold fingers. 'Take one thing at a time, and let's hope, first of all, that the operation is successful.' She drew Margot down on to the small leather sofa and sat down beside her. 'Is there anything I can do for you? Anything I could get you?'

Joanne Grant's sincere concern sent a rush of warmth through Margot, and it triggered off the frightened tears she had held in check since hearing the news of her mother's collapse, but she swallowed convulsively and blinked away the moisture in her eyes before whispering unsteadily, 'There's n-nothing, thank you.'

The minutes dragged into yet another hour in that small waiting-room which was shut off from the hum of activity in the rest of the hospital, but the waiting had become bearable in Joanne's company. Her calm, unruffled presence had had the desired effect on Margot's taut nerves until the sound of approaching footsteps caused Margot to leap anxiously to her feet.

'Your mother is being taken to a private ward,' Dr Turner told Margot after a brief, acknowledging smile in Joanne's direction. 'The operation itself was a success, but we still have to wait for the results from the Path. Lab.'

'May I see her?' Margot asked at once, her voice shaky with relief.

'Not just at the moment, but I'll show you to the waiting-room close to her ward.'

A light hand on her arm checked Margot as she was about to follow Dr Turner's fatherly figure from the room.

'I'll call back again later,' Joanne smiled, and Margot

leaned forward impulsively to kiss her on the cheek.

'Thank you ... for everything.'

It was some considerable time before Margot was allowed in to see her mother, and even then she found her heavily sedated, but she remained seated in a chair close to the bed, and only vaguely conscious of the nursing Sister who had been assigned to take special care of her mother. Dr Turner, too, drifted in and out from time to time, but Margot's anxious eyes remained riveted to the pale, almost painfully thin figure lying so quietly on the high hospital bed. It seemed at times as if she were not breathing, but a steady flow of plasma was being fed into her veins while the instruments monitored her pulse and respiratory rate. This was nothing new to Margot, but it seemed frightening, somehow, to see all those wires and tubes attached to her mother's unconscious form.

Margot had no concept of time as she sat there. A meal had been brought in to her on a tray, but it had been returned to the kitchen untouched despite Dr Turner's frowning displeasure.

Joanne Grant's arrival could not, however, be ignored in the same manner. With one swift glance about the room she assessed the situation and, turning to Margot, she said unexpectedly, 'Come home with me now and spend the night with us.'

Margot stared at her mother's white face against the pillows and shook her head. 'I'd prefer to stay here.'

'Why don't you accept Mrs Grant's invitation, Margot, and get some rest,' Dr Turner intervened sensibly. 'It would be foolish for both you *and* me to wait around here, and I'll ring through to Mrs Grant's home the moment there's a noticeable change in your mother's condition.'

'I don't want to inconvenience you, Joanne,' Margot persisted stubbornly. 'I'll be perfectly all right at my own home.'

'Nonsense!' Joanne whispered sharply in an authoritative voice. 'You can't possibly stay there all on your own, and most especially not tonight.'

Margot could no longer deny the tiredness seeping into her limbs, and the thought of spending the night in a quiet, empty house suddenly lost its attraction for her. Glancing up at Joanne, she capitulated. 'I'll just touch in at my home, then, to collect a few things, and ... thank you.'

'I haven't done anything yet to deserve your thanks,' Joanne smiled, taking Margot's hands and drawing her up out of her chair. 'Come on, my dear. Your mother looks quite peaceful, and Dr Turner and the Sister here will watch over her like hawks.'

Margot glanced at Dr Turner and asked urgently, 'You will promise to ring me if there's any change?'

'The moment there's a development,' he promised, and, satisfied, she accompanied Joanne from the hospital.

The house seemed strange and oppressive without her mother there to welcome her, and Margot hurriedly changed out of her uniform into something warmer. She packed a few things into a small suitcase, and a little more than a half hour later she was being ushered into Joanne's spaciously modern kitchen. The electric clock against the wall told her that it was after eight and, coming in out of the cold, dark night, Margot found the kitchen bright and warm.

'Have you had anything to eat this evening?' Joanne asked, and when she saw the expression that flitted across Margot's pale, drawn features, she smiled and said: 'I know that food is the furthest thing from your mind at the moment, but I left a helping of stew in the oven for you, and there's soup if you'd like some.'

'Just stew will do, thank you,' Margot assured her as she seated herself tiredly at the circular pinewood table. 'I'm not very hungry.'

She forced herself to eat the first few mouthsful of food in an effort to satisfy Joanne, but a few minutes later she was eating hungrily, and it came as somewhat of a surprise to recall that she had had nothing to eat since breakfast that morning.

When Margot finally rose from the table to wash and dry her plate, she caught Joanne's smiling glance resting on her, and her own lips curved into a faintly guilty smile as she said selfconsciously, 'That was lovely, thanks. I never realised that I was this hungry.'

'Your mother is going to be in hospital for quite some time, and while she's there I would like you to consider this your home,' Joanne announced while she poured two cups of coffee and joined Margot at the table.

'Oh, no, I couldn't!' Margot protested at once, startled by this unexpected offer. 'It's kind of you to make the suggestion, Joanne, but I wouldn't dream of inconveniencing you to that extent.'

'It wouldn't be an inconvenience,' Joanne argued. 'I would love you to stay.'

'But I have a home.'

'You can't possibly stay there all on your own. You'd find yourself brooding over all kinds of things, and you'd be making yourself thoroughly miserable,' Joanne continued to argue sensibly, then the sound of a step at the door made her glance up imploringly at the man who had just entered the kitchen. 'Daniel, *you* talk to her. Tell her it would be silly to go home every night to an empty house while her mother's in hospital when there's plenty of room here for her.'

Daniel Grant, his lean body unfamiliarly clad in corded pants and thick woollen sweater, frowned down at Margot from his great height. 'Joanne is right,' he said, 'and it would make us happy if you would accept.'

'But I——' Margot faltered, torn between the desire to maintain her independence and the desire for company, but she decided on the latter when her troubled glance met Joanne's steady gaze. 'You—you're both very kind,' she said haltingly, 'and I—I'd like to stay very much.'

'That's settled, then,' Joanne announced delightedly, clasping Margot's hands across the table with a reassuring pressure.

'Serena is restless,' Daniel interrupted this touching scene. 'I think you'd better go upstairs and take a look, Lorelei.'

'Oh, dear,' Joanne smiled ruefully, rising at once to her feet. 'Help yourself to more coffee, Margot, and excuse me, will you?'

'I suggest you take a few days off from work until your mother is out of danger,' Daniel suggested the moment they were alone.

'Oh, no, please, Dr Grant,' Margot protested at once. 'I would prefer to be kept busy rather than sitting about idle and worrying myself silly.'

He seated himself in the chair Joanne had vacated and lit a cigarette while he observed Margot through narrowed blue eyes. 'Theatre work demands absolute concentration and under the present circumstances...'

'I know,' she replied instantly when he left his sentence unfinished. 'I shan't fail you, Dr Grant.'

'I don't doubt your capabilities, Margot,' he stated with absolute sincerity. 'I'm merely considering your state of mind at the moment.'

She understood perfectly. As Chief Surgeon he could not afford to have someone like herself in the theatre whose mind was elsewhere and not on her job, but she was determined to be at her post the next day.

'If I find that I'm unable to cope, then I'll do as you suggest and take a few days off.'

'Good girl,' he said abruptly, his stern features relaxing into a smile, then the chime of the doorbell made him push back his chair and rise to his feet. 'Excuse me.'

Left alone, Margot helped herself to a second cup of coffee, and tried to relax, but her mother's pale features swam disturbingly before her eyes. What would they find in the tumour they had removed? she wondered anxiously and, as the possibility of cancer raised its viperous head in her thoughts, she groaned softly and buried her face in her hands. She could not bear thinking about it, and yet she could not shut out the frightening thought.

'Margot?' The resonant timbre of that deep, familiar voice made her look up sharply to find Jordan standing beside her, his dark, unfathomable glance resting on her pale features. 'How is your mother?'

Margot swallowed nervously. They had not parted on the friendliest terms the day before, and his manner in the theatre that afternoon had conveyed the future trend of their relationship, yet here he was, behaving as if nothing had happened, and confusing her still further with an unmistakable display of concern.

'My mother has survived the operation,' she told him, suspicion placing her on her guard. 'That's just about all I can tell you at the moment.'

He pulled out the chair nearest to her and sat down, his glance taking in the thickness and sheen of her russet-coloured hair as it tumbled about her face and shoulders. 'I'd like to apologise for my abruptness in the theatre earlier today.'

'That's understandable,' she replied, attempting to be generous despite her bewilderment.

'Margot . . .' He paused and clasped her hand in his, but his touch awakened memories that were still too disturbingly fresh in her mind, and she jerked her hand free.

'Please!' she said stiffly, making an effort to control her wayward pulse. 'Your interest in my mother's health is touching, but there's no need for you to concern yourself.'

'This isn't the time for arguments resulting from personal differences and prejudices, Margot,' he reprimanded sharply, and when her wide blue glance met his curiously, he added: 'Let's call a truce and start afresh.'

Her body stiffened with suspicion. 'Start afresh in what way, Dr Merrick? What exactly do you have in mind?'

'I would say we could start by being civil to each other, and let things go on from there,' he suggested, and although the suggestion appealed to her immensely, she had no intention of allowing things to develop as far as they had before.

'Civility costs nothing, I suppose,' she agreed at last, 'and it might be wise to call a truce considering that we have to work together almost every day, but let's keep it strictly professional.'

'If you say so, Sister Huntley.'

'Don't mock me, Dr Merrick,' she retorted sharply,

catching a glimpse of devilment lurking in his eyes.

'We called a truce, remember?' he reminded her, extending his hand. 'Do we shake on it?'

Margot hesitated, but only briefly, then she nodded and placed her hand in his. It would be so much simpler to be friends rather than enemies, she decided, and it was at this point that Joanne walked into the kitchen.

'It's time you got some rest, Margot,' she announced, and, glancing at Jordan, she added: 'Daniel is waiting for you in the study.'

'Thanks, Joanne,' Jordan smiled briefly, but when he rose to his feet he turned once more to Margot. 'See you tomorrow,' he said, and moments later she was alone in the kitchen with Joanne.

'Come with me, my dear,' she invited, linking her arm through Margot's and drawing her towards the door. 'Your suitcase is upstairs.'

In the guestroom, furnished in warm autumn shades, Margot turned to face the woman beside her and found those green eyes regarding her with a friendly warmth that touched her cold heart. 'Joanne . . . I don't know how to thank you.'

'Then don't,' Joanne smiled. 'Just get some rest, and try not to worry. If you should want anything during the night, then don't hesitate to call us. We're three doors down from you.' Her lips brushed Margot's cheek. 'Goodnight, my dear.'

Margot slept fitfully that night, and she was up and dressed before dawn the following morning in order to call on at the hospital before she reported for duty at the clinic. She went quietly down the carpeted stairs, but when she entered the kitchen she found that Joanne had beaten her to it. Dressed in a warm housecoat, she turned from the stove to smile at Margot.

'I heard you moving about when I passed your room a few minutes ago, so I decided to get your breakfast ready. Besides . . .' she added hurriedly, almost anticipating Margot's protestations as she gestured with a slender hand towards the chubby little girl seated in the feeding chair beside the table, 'Serena is hungry, and I'm told I make a terrific omelette.'

Margot shook her head in silent wonder, and decided that it would be futile to argue that she was not hungry when the delicious aroma of cheese omelettes was already making her mouth water, so she put down her handbag and draped her cape over the back of her chair before she sat down beside the year-old baby in the high chair.

Serena had her mother's golden-brown hair, Margot decided, but she had her father's blue eyes, and they were, at that precise moment, regarding Margot with a great deal of curiosity and wariness. A wet little finger was finally extended to tentatively explore the epaulette with its designatory badges on Margot's shoulder, but the ice was broken when Margot reciprocated by tickling her lightly beneath the chin. The child gurgled with laughter, and Margot would have had to possess a heart of stone not to join in.

'Serena . . .' Margot murmured absently. 'You have a lovely name, Serena.'

'She was named after Daniel's mother,' Joanne explained, placing Margot's omelette in front of her and pulling up a chair to feed the child. 'Serena Grant was a wonderful woman,' Joanne continued. 'She was serene as her name suggested, but she was also one of the most courageous women I've ever known.' Her eyes grew misty with reminiscent thoughts, but that look was replaced swiftly with a humorous smile. 'I can only hope that Serena takes after her grandmother, but at the moment she shows every sign of being exactly the opposite.'

'I take it that Dr Grant's mother is no longer alive?'

'She died of cancer a few months after Daniel and I were married,' Joanne explained while shovelling porridge into the child's hungry little mouth. 'She was a straightforward person, almost blunt at times, but I loved her "don't fuss and fidget" attitude, and I missed her terribly when she was no longer there.'

*When she was no longer there.* Those words echoed repeatedly through Margot's mind when she drove herself to the hospital some time later. What would she do when her mother was no longer there? she wondered at length, but the thought did not bear thinking about, and she drew a deep, steadying breath when she finally parked the Mini and hurried into the hospital.

'How is she?' she wanted to know when she entered the silent ward to find Dr Turner bending over her mother's prostrate form.

'Ask her yourself,' he suggested with a smile as he glanced at Margot over his shoulder and moved away from the bed.

'Mum?' Margot whispered a little hesitantly as she approached her, but when those grey eyes looked directly up into hers she could have wept with relief. 'Oh, Mum, I've been so worried about you!'

'Silly girl,' Beryl smiled tiredly, and when Margot leaned over her to kiss her, she added: 'I'm sorry about all this fuss.'

'No one's fussing,' Margot laughed, but her laughter sounded choked as the tears rose in her throat. 'Just get well, for my sake.'

'I'll try,' her mother sighed, 'but I'm so desperately tired.'

'Then close your eyes and rest as much as you can,' Margot suggested. 'I'll call in again during my lunch hour.'

Surprisingly, her mother obeyed, and Margot remained beside her bed a few moments longer until Dr Turner signalled that he wished to speak to her privately. Leaving the Sister in charge, he accompanied Margot down the passage towards the exit.

'What have you heard?' she asked anxiously when they were some distance from her mother's ward.

Dr Turner glanced at her swiftly, then away again. 'The Path. Lab, results show that the tumour was cancerous.'

'Oh, oh, no!' Margot felt as if she had been caught up in an icy blast of wind which had swept down from the mountain. 'Has it spread, do you think?'

'That's difficult to say,' Dr Turner frowned. 'We'll be doing a series of tests on her, but at the moment I can't give you any definite information beyond what I've already told you.'

'She's not very strong.'

'She's survived the operation, and that gives us every reason to believe that there's hope yet,' Dr Turner smiled reassuringly when they stood on the steps outside the building. 'We'll do our best, Margot.'

'I know you will,' she replied, forcing her lips into an answering smile, but her heart had become chilled with fear at the thought of what lay ahead.

She had time to compose herself during the drive up to the clinic, but she had been in the nursing profession long enough to know that the removal of a cancerous tumour did not necessarily result in total recovery for the unfortunate patient. She had to face facts, and facing them meant accepting that there was a strong possibility that the cancer could have spread. It was an unacceptable thought, but it might well be inevitable.

'Any news?' Jordan asked, coming into her office soon after her arrival, and alerting her dulled senses to his sheer masculinity.

'The tumour was malignant,' she replied, forcing a casualness into her voice as she handed him the schedule for the day, but he barely glanced at it before flicking it back on to her desk.

'How far has it spread?'

'They don't know for sure, but they intend finding out.'

Their eyes met, but when the heat of tears stung her eyelids, she turned hastily towards her desk and made a pretence of tidying it.

'Don't lose hope, Margot.'

'Hope is all I've got at the moment,' she sighed despairingly, making an effort to steady herself, then heavy hands came down on to her shoulders, and their pressure was oddly comforting as Jordan turned her about to face him.

'Do you feel up to a stint in the theatre?' he asked with abrupt concern.

'I'm ready whenever you are, Dr Merrick.'

Her voice sounded coldly professional, but it was, at that moment, a barrier behind which to hide her feelings, and when Jordan's hands fell away from her shoulders his features were expressionless. He inclined his head in her direction, then turned on his heel and walked out of her office.

The abrupt change in his manner puzzled her. Had she perhaps offended him in some way? she wondered vaguely, but she had no time to deliberate on the subject as she hastened to prepare herself mentally and physically for the long hours of surgery ahead. She had given Daniel Grant her word, and she fully intended keeping it. She would not fail him, or the clinic.

# CHAPTER FIVE

MARGOT prayed that she would never have to endure another day such as the one she had just been through. After the long hours of concentration in the theatre that morning, she had rushed off during her lunch hour to see her mother, but when she found her resting peacefully she left again quietly to face another three-hour session in the operating theatre with Daniel Grant this time.

When she left the clinic late that afternoon, she touched down at the hospital once more to find her mother awake and slightly more lucid, but she had still complained of immense tiredness and pain.

Margot had never before felt so totally helpless, nor so terribly afraid, and her mother's sickly pallor had merely increased her concern to the point of desperation.

There was no sense in staying, the Sister in charge had told Margot when her mother had dropped off to sleep once more. Dr Turner and Dr Russell would soon be in to check on Beryl's condition, the Sister had added, and in the meantime everything possible was being done for her.

Margot could not fault the Sister on the latter. Everything possible *was* being done for her mother, but she remained oddly reluctant to leave until she finally allowed herself to be persuaded that there was no sense in remaining at her mother's side. After one last look at those beloved features she drove herself home to change out of her uniform and to collect a few extra items of clothing, then she returned to the house up on the hill that bordered on the Merrick property.

'How is your mother?' Joanne asked at once when Margot walked into their living-room to find Jordan, drink in hand, standing beside the fireplace with Daniel, and their conversation ceased at once as they turned to focus their attention on Margot.

'She's tired, and not very talkative,' she replied, glancing only briefly at Jordan. 'There's no further news at present.'

'These things take time,' Daniel warned, handing her a glass of wine when she had seated herself in the chair beside Joanne's.

'I know,' Margot smiled faintly, but the smile was replaced by a frown a moment later, and she caught her quivering lip between her teeth to steady it. 'If only she weren't so weak,' she explained.

The wine steadied her considerably, but the shrill ring of the telephone in the hall jarred against her sensitive nerves and filled her with a premonition of something that she was not yet ready to face. In silence they waited while Joanne went to answer it, but, when she returned a few seconds later, Margot knew at once that something was terribly wrong.

'Margot . . .' Joanne began hesitantly, then the rest came out in a sympathetic rush. 'I think you'd better get back to the hospital. It sounds urgent.'

Margot was on her feet at once, fear churning through her at a sickening pace as she pulled on her suede coat and headed for the door, but Jordan was beside her before she reached it.

'I'll take you,' he said, and Margot did not have the strength nor the will to argue when he gripped her arm and ushered her out to his waiting car.

The Mercedes leapt into action, moving at a speed which would have had her clutching nervously at her seat had it not been for the burning anxiety within her to reach her destination as swiftly as possible, and less than ten minutes later they were entering the hospital through the swinging glass doors.

'Sister Huntley?' a young nurse asked tentatively as she approached them, then her eyes lit up with appreciation as she took in the tall, silent man at Margot's side, and it seemed, for a moment, as if she had forgotten the reason for her presence in the foyer.

'Yes?' Margot snapped impatiently. 'What's happened?'

The young nurse made an obvious effort to pull herself together before she addressed Margot. 'Mrs Huntley has developed an internal haemorrhage. Dr Russell and Dr Turner are with her now in the theatre,' she explained, then she indicated towards a small waiting-room close by. 'If you would like to wait in here, then Dr Turner will see you as soon as he can possibly manage it.'

Jordan thanked the nurse abruptly, then his hand on Margot's arm tightened as he steered her into the bleak waiting-room with its upright, uncomfortable chairs, and its sad-looking fern on a wooden stand beside the window.

'Jordan?' she began frantically, tormenting herself with the most terrifying visions.

'Get a hold on yourself,' Jordan ordered sharply, his hands gripping her shoulders and shaking her slightly. 'They're doing everything they possibly can for her.'

'I know,' she replied in a choked voice, regaining her control with an effort before she risked raising her glance to meet those dark, unfathomable eyes. 'I'm sorry.'

'Sit down,' he said abruptly, pushing her into a chair and seating himself beside her with his long, muscled legs stretched out in front of him.

'Jordan, what if——'

'What if *nothing*,' he interrupted sharply. 'She's not the first patient to suffer a post-operative internal hae-morrhage, and she won't be the last.'

That was true, of course, Margot admitted to herself as she gnawed away at her bottom lip, but it was a different matter entirely when the patient was one's own mother. If Beryl Huntley had been a strong, healthy woman, Margot might not have been so terribly con-cerned, but she had grown frail and weak over the past months, and after the lengthy operation the day before it would be a miracle if she managed to survive this setback.

It seemed as though they had waited there in silence for hours instead of forty-five minutes before the sound of approaching footsteps made her rise from her chair, and she glanced expectantly towards the door which stood slightly ajar. Dr Turner, still dressed in his green theatre gown, entered the room, but one look at the grim expression on his tired, drawn features made her realise that what she had dreaded most had happened, and her blood seemed to flow like iced water through her veins.

'It's over, isn't it?' she heard herself say in a husky voice that sounded quite unlike her own. 'She—she's gone, isn't she?'

Dr Turner nodded tiredly and explained. 'Every-thing was going smoothly. We'd stopped the haemor-rhage, then she suffered a cardiac arrest. We tried everything possible, but . . .'

He left his sentence unfinished, his bushy eyebrows meeting in a frown as if he were mentally going over every incident he had lived through in the theatre while seeking an explanation for what had occurred.

'May I see her?' Margot asked quietly, a curious numbness taking possession of her.

Dr Turner glanced at Jordan as if seeking his approval, then he nodded slowly. 'Come this way.'

Later, in the passage just outside the recovery room which adjoined the operating theatre, Margot indicated that she wanted to go in alone, and the two men remained behind when she entered the small, familiar room with its antiseptic smell and stark white walls. The nurses in attendance vanished discreetly as she approached the centre of the room where a silent figure lay prostrate on a trolley, and Margot was vaguely surprised at the remarkable steadiness of her hands when she drew back the sheet to look down upon her mother's still form. The grey eyes were closed for ever, and the white, translucent skin was smooth, the lines of pain and wariness no longer visible. She looked peaceful and oddly young, Margot thought as she calmly brushed a light hand over the greying head, then she raised the sheet to cover those still features and walked out of the room.

Jordan was there, silent and strong, and his hand was firm beneath her elbow when he escorted her out of the hospital building. She shivered as the coldness followed them into his car, then her control snapped and, to her dismay, hot tears rolled unchecked down her cheeks. She must have made some sort of sound, for he turned towards her at once, and the next moment she was clamped against his broad chest, his arms hard and comforting about her while she wept unrestrainedly into his shoulder.

'Forgive me,' she said at last, stirring in the haven of his arms and accepting the handkerchief he offered her. 'I—I didn't intend to make such a spectacle of myself.'

'Under the circumstances it's understandable,' he said quietly, his eyes searching her white face in the darkness. 'Feeling better?'

'Y—Yes,' she replied unsteadily from behind the white linen of his handkerchief. 'Thank you.'

Margot remembered very little of the drive back to the Grant home that evening, but when they arrived there she found that the news of her mother's death had somehow preceded her. Joanne took charge of the situation in her gentle, compassionate way, while Daniel pressed a glass into her hand and ordered her to drink the amber-coloured contents. It smelled obnoxious and tasted vile, but it steadied her within seconds and sent a welcome warmth surging into her cold, shaky limbs.

Jordan refused Joanne's invitation to stay to dinner and he left a few minutes later, but that night, while Margot lay awake in bed and alone with her sorrow, she found herself longing once again for the comforting strength of Jordan's arms. It was madness, that sense of belonging she had experienced while he had held her, but at that moment she felt like a piece of driftwood cut loose from its moorings, and in desperate need of a safe anchorage.

'There's so much to do that I hardly know where to begin,' Margot complained the following morning, but Joanne merely smiled and shook her head.

'There's nothing for you to do, Margot,' she said quietly. 'Everything is being taken care of.'

'And I don't want to see you at the clinic until you feel up to it,' Daniel added authoritatively across the breakfast table. 'I told you last night that you could take off the rest of this week, but you may stretch it into two weeks if you feel the need for it.'

Their kindness enveloped her like a warm cloak during the next few days. Jordan was there too, and his presence was like a steady rock, supporting her during those moments when she so desperately needed someone to lean on. As Joanne had said, everything had been taken care of, and the morning after the funeral, when Margot joined Joanne on the sun porch for tea, she tried to express her appreciation.

'You and Daniel have both been so very kind,' she began unsteadily. 'I don't know how to thank you for making all the necessary arrangements for the funeral, and——'

'We didn't make the arrangements, Margot,' Joanne interrupted calmly. 'It's Jordan you have to thank for that.'

'Jordan?' Margot stared incredulously at the woman seated opposite her in the cane chair. 'But I—I don't understand. Why should he—I never thought—Oh, my goodness!'

It had never occurred to her that Jordan was the one to thank for relieving her of those painful duties, but she understood now why he had always been there when she had needed him most. He had taken command, quietly and unobtrusively, and in the most unexpected way imaginable.

'Don't let it worry you, Margot,' Joanne interrupted her disturbed thoughts. 'Like most men Jordan enjoyed taking charge of the situation.'

Margot digested this information with difficulty.

Jordan had not only taken charge of the situation, but he had taken charge of her heart as well, and admitting this to herself was a painful experience she could have done without at that moment.

'I shall have to start thinking of returning to my own home,' she said at length, trying to alter the trend of her thoughts.

'Not yet, Margot,' Joanne protested at once. 'Stay a while longer—at least until the end of the week.'

Margot shook her head decisively. 'It doesn't pay to put off the inevitable. I have to go back there some time, and the sooner the better.'

'I suppose you're right,' Joanne grimaced, 'but I'm going to miss not having you about, and Serena is going to miss your spoiling.'

Serena gurgled as if in agreement as she walked unsteadily towards Margot, and she scooped the child up into her arms, hugging her close and allowing her to play with the beads about her neck until something else caught Serena's attention, then she wriggled down off Margot's lap and toddled off to investigate.

'You've been wonderful, Joanne. I'll never be able to thank you enough,' said Margot, her eyes following the child's unsteady progress across the sun porch.

'Then don't try,' Joanne laughed lightly, filling their tea-cups a second time, and adding teasingly, 'It would only make me blush.'

Margot returned to her home that same day; to the silence and the emptiness, and the heartbreakingly familiar objects which had belonged to her mother. Her personality lingered in every room, while crocheted centres and embroidered cloths served as reminders of the deftness of those slender fingers. A thin layer of dust covered the furniture and, choking back the hot tears,

Margot set to work. Airing and cleaning the house gave her something to do, and she worked slowly, stretching out each task to last until it was time for her to go to bed.

She sat down to a lonely meal that evening, and forced herself to eat it, then she rinsed the dishes, wiped the cupboards, and washed the floor, but by eight o'clock she was left with nothing more to do. It was too early to go to bed, so she picked up a magazine and tried to read, but the words jumbled senselessly before her eyes. She switched on the kettle at last, and stood staring into the darkness beyond the small window, but the wind whistled around the corners of the house and, shivering, she drew the curtains across the window in an attempt to shut out the loneliness of the night, and the dreadful silence which was broken only by the occasional creaking of the iron roof. She realised, for the first time, that over the years her mother had stood in for her father and the family they had never had, and now, suddenly, she was left with nothing. She was alone; completely alone and, in that moment of miserable self-pity and immense sorrow, she did not check the tears as they flowed hot and fast down her cheeks.

The kettle whistled and the doorbell rang simultaneously and, dashing away her tears with the back of her hand, she switched off the kettle and walked quickly down the passage towards the front door.

'Who is it?' she asked anxiously through the door.

'Jordan,' came the reply at once. 'May I come in?'

'Yes—yes, of course,' she said unsteadily, hastily repairing some of the damage to her face with her fingertips before she unlocked the door and let him in, but her efforts were in vain, for his razor-sharp glance was quick to detect the unusual brightness of her eyes and the dampness on her thick, dark lashes.

'Have you been crying?' he asked unnecessarily.

'A little,' she admitted, closing the door to shut out the cold and leading the way into the kitchen. 'I was going to make myself a cup of coffee. Would you like to join me?'

'I shan't say no,' he replied, pulling out a chair and seating himself at the table. 'Are you going to continue living here on your own?'

'It's my home,' she reminded him accusingly without turning from her task, and Jordan did not pursue the subject as he watched her set out the cups and pour the coffee.

It was a relief for Margot to have someone there with her, even if only for a short while, to break the deathly silence which only her activities had disturbed slightly. Her mother's bedroom door was still closed, however, and Margot did not yet have the necessary courage to enter it. Perhaps, in a week or so, when the shock of her mother's death and the pain of her loss had subsided slightly, she would find herself strong enough to sort through her mother's personal belongings.

She handed Jordan his coffee and joined him at the table, but when she wrapped her cold fingers around her coffee mug, she recalled the conversation she had had with Joanne that morning, and she looked up, straight into those disturbing eyes. Disconcerted, she lowered her glance, and stumbled into an unrehearsed speech.

'I—I believe you made all the necessary arrangements for—for my mother's funeral. I——' Her throat worked with the effort to control the tears which were so perilously close to the surface. 'I scarcely know how to begin to—to thank you, but I hope I—I shall be able to repay you some day.'

There was an awkward little silence before he said slowly, 'It was my privilege and my pleasure, and you can thank me by never mentioning repayment again.'

'You've been very kind,' she murmured, still unable to meet his glance, then Jordan changed the subject abruptly.

'I believe you're going to return to the clinic on Monday.'

'That's right.'

'Good,' he muttered, glowering down at his mug of coffee. 'Sister Lewis has filled the breach admirably, but as a team we were a disaster.'

'Do I sense a compliment hidden somewhere in that remark?' she asked with a faint touch of humour in her voice.

'Could be,' he smiled lazily, and they lapsed into a surprisingly comfortable silence while they drank their coffee, then he set aside his empty cup and said frowningly, 'I know this is a touchy subject, but I don't like the idea of your living here alone in this house.'

'Good heavens, Jordan,' she replied, her voice sharper than she had intended, 'I'm quite capable of taking care of myself, you know.'

'Are you?'

His eyes glittered strangely as they travelled over her, taking in the well-worn baggy sweater which did not quite succeed in hiding the agitated rise and fall of her rounded breasts. An unwanted intimacy had slipped into their conversation, and in an attempt to ward it off she pushed back her chair and rose to her feet.

'More coffee?' she asked, endeavouring to swing the situation back on to a safer level.

'If you want me to stay longer, yes.'

'Jordan . . .' she began, turning to face him with a

sharp reply hovering on her tongue, but the words remained lodged in her throat when she found him standing so close to her that his masculine scent invaded her nostrils and stirred her numbed senses. His nearness had been comforting during the past few days, but at that moment it was breathtakingly sensual and, vulnerable as she was, it was a dangerous situation to find herself in. His eyes held hers captive with a paralysing magnetism that made her realise just how helpless she would be in his arms with that sensual, often cynical mouth against her own, and the mere thought of such intimacy between them sent the blood flowing rapidly through her veins. 'Please...' she begged frantically when she managed to find her voice, and it sounded decidedly faint above the wild hammering of her heart. 'Don't make things difficult for me.'

His straight, dark brows rose mockingly. 'In what way do you mean?'

'You know very well what I mean,' she cried exasperatedly, too afraid to move for fear of coming into contact with his body.

'For heaven's sake, Margot!' The words fell harshly from his lips, and his hands bit deep into her shoulders as he dragged her up against him. Her body grew taut, preparing to resist the onslaught of his kisses, but what she feared did not happen, and he thrust her aside almost as if she had disgusted him. 'Lock the door behind me, and go to bed,' he ordered in a tight-lipped fashion. 'Perhaps you'll be in a better frame of mind tomorrow.'

Guilt, after all he had done for her, sent her rushing after him as he strode from the kitchen, and she managed to catch up with him before he reached the front door.

'Jordan!' He turned, his eyes boring down into hers,

and she bit her lip nervously. 'I'm sorry,' she said lamely.

For a moment he stood immovable like a rock, then, without warning, she was swept up into his arms and kissed with a thoroughness that left her flushed and trembling. He was gone before she could berate him, and her hands shook visibly when she locked the door and flicked the safety catch into position. Later, when she lay on her bed staring into the darkness, she wished with all her heart that she could hate him, but she knew that she could never do that. Never—not as long as she lived.

As the days lengthened into weeks an odd relationship developed between Margot and Jordan which she could only describe as a wary friendship. He came to see her often, occasionally staying for dinner, and she finally relinquished her attempts to keep him at bay when she discovered that she found his company intensely stimulating. They talked about many things, but their conversation remained on an impersonal level, and instead of dreading his visits, she had to admit with some reluctance that she looked forward to them.

At the clinic Margot treated Jordan with the respect and admiration he deserved and, except for Daniel and Joanne Grant, she took great care that no one should suspect, or begin to speculate about their relationship. Nothing would come of it, after all, for she continually reminded herself that they belonged on different sides of the tracks, but it became increasingly difficult to ignore those painful little jabs in the region of her heart.

Margot arrived home late one Friday afternoon to the sound of the telephone ringing in the passage and, unsuspectingly, she hurried inside to answer it.

'Margot?' a vaguely familiar voice queried abruptly, and a frown settled between Margot's brows.

'Yes, that's right.'

'Eva Merrick,' that abrupt voice enlightened her, and an unpleasant little tremor rippled through Margot. 'Are you free tomorrow morning?'

'Yes, I am, Mrs Merrick. Why?'

'If you'll meet me at the Protea Tea Room tomorrow morning then I'll explain everything.'

'But, Mrs Merrick, I——'

'Will ten-thirty suit you?' that autocratic voice demanded.

'Yes, but I——'

'I'll see you then,' Eva Merrick interrupted, 'and please be punctual.'

The line went dead before Margot could question her further, and she returned the receiver to its cradle with an angry exclamation on her lips. What on earth could Eva Merrick want with her? she wondered with half a mind not to meet her, but she knew that her curiosity would not allow her to stay away.

The Protea Tea Room was the only respectable place in Willowmead where one could order a drinkable pot of tea and freshly baked scones, but Margot was certain that this had nothing to do with Eva Merrick's choice of rendezvous. It simply meant that they would meet each other on neutral ground for whatever purpose the autocratic old lady had in mind, and Margot was not fooled into thinking that Eva Merrick was merely desirous of her company.

Punctual to the very second, Margot arrived at the tea room the Saturday morning to find Jordan's mother waiting for her at a corner table. Their tea was served the moment Margot was seated and Eva Merrick, the lacy cuffs of her blouse protruding from the sleeves of her expensive linen suit, poured their tea as if she were handling delicate china instead of stainless steel and inexpensive pottery.

'I won't waste time on trivialities, so I shall come straight to the point,' she said, passing Margot her tea. 'I realise, of course, that working together, as you and Jordan do, you are bound to see each other often, but I also happen to know that you have been seeing each other privately and quite consistently over the past weeks.'

Margot only barely managed to conceal her surprise. 'Mrs Merrick, we've——'

'Please allow me to finish,' the older woman interrupted imperiously. 'The seven years in Europe have not altered Jordan, and I would like to issue a word of warning. He will continue to sow his wild oats, as they say, although his choice of feminine company often leaves much to be desired, but that will change shortly when his engagement to Berdine Powell is announced.' The precision-aimed arrows found their mark, and Eva Merrick smiled with obvious satisfaction when she saw the colour drain from Margot's face. 'Berdine is from a wealthy and highly respected family in Cape Town, and we're expecting her to arrive tomorrow on a short visit during which they will naturally decide on the wedding date.' Those thin lips curved with cruel, almost sadistic pleasure as she twisted the arrows in Margot's heart. 'You do understand why I'm telling you this, don't you?'

It was several seconds before Margot was able to control herself sufficiently to speak, and then pride dictated the words she uttered. 'I do understand, Mrs Merrick,' she said coldly, 'but you have nothing to fear

from me. I've always known my place, and I can also
assure you that I have no personal interest whatsoever
in your son. He's been very kind to me since my mother
died, but there's nothing between us that need cause
you the slightest concern.'

'May I hope, then, that you will bring this affair between you to an immediate end?'

Margot went white about the mouth. 'We are not
lovers, Mrs Merrick, merely friends, but I shall make
it very clear to Jordan in future that his presence is not
desired.'

'Thank you,' the older woman smiled, sipping
daintily at her tea while those cold eyes observed
Margot intently. 'I knew you would be reasonable
about this.'

'It's my pleasure, Mrs Merrick,' Margot replied with
as much iciness as she could muster.

'Your tea must be cold,' Jordan's mother remarked
with sickening sweetness. 'Shall I pour you another?'

'No, thank you,' Margot replied, picking up her
handbag, 'and I would be grateful if you would excuse
me, Mrs Merrick. I still have plenty to do before the
shops close this morning.'

Eva Merrick nodded her regal head, and Margot
marched out of the tea room with her head held high,
and her heart filled with lead.

She waded doggedly through her shopping list, not
giving herself time to think, or feel, until she entered her
home and dumped her parcels on to the kitchen table,
then, in her mother's bedroom, where her favourite per-
fume still clung to the items of clothing Margot had not
had the heart to discard, she wept soul-wrenching tears
that did very little to alleviate her aching misery.

She had been a fool! An imbecile! She had suspected

for some time that Jordan was merely using her to fill in time, but instead of shutting him out of her life she had let him in, and, as a result, she had laid herself wide open to pain and disillusionment.

Margot nursed the fierce hope that she would never have to see Jordan again other than in the operating theatre, but on the Sunday afternoon, when she had least expected it, she opened her door to find him standing on the threshold.

Knowing the truth, she found his audacity beyond her comprehension and, her well-rehearsed speech forgotten, she demanded angrily, 'What do you want?'

'I could answer that question if you'd invite me in.'

'I'm busy, and I don't want——' She broke off sharply when the door was thrust aside, taking her with it, then it was wrenched from her hands and slammed shut. Afraid, but not subdued, she stared up into his mutinous face and demanded angrily, 'What do you think you're doing?'

'Since when has my welcome expired?' he counter-questioned harshly.

'Since today.'

'Explain yourself.'

She felt his anger, like a force vibrating through her, and cautioned herself to take care. 'Your kindness and consideration has been appreciated, but it's time the situation returned to normal.'

'Normal?' he thundered, and she shrank back against the wall as he towered over her menacingly. 'No, I dare say the situation has not been normal these past weeks. Every time I've been with you I've had the greatest difficulty in suppressing my natural instincts and desires; desires such as *this*, for instance.'

One moment his eyes were blazing down into hers,

and the next his arms were pinning her to the length of his body, her breasts hurting against his hard chest, and her lips crushed beneath the punishing force of his mouth. At first she was too stunned to react, then she struggled against him and succeeded in wrenching her mouth from his. She dragged the air into her tortured lungs and spread her fingers wide against his chest in a futile effort to push him away, but his hand fastened on to the nape of her neck, and there was no escape for her after that.

'No!' she gasped pleadingly. 'You can't do this to me!'

'Yes, I can, Margot!' he breathed mockingly, and the smile of the devil was on his lips befoore his mouth swooped down to claim hers.

His kiss was no longer punishing, but a sensual and tantalising exploration of her mouth that made her senses reel crazily. She tried desperately not to respond, reminding herself that he was merely using her while intending to make someone else his wife, but her resistance was crumbling like a cardboard house in the breeze. She tried to stop him when his fingers tugged at the zip down the front of her warm housecoat, but, when she felt the sensual pressure of his hand against the rounded swell of her breast, the final fragments of her control snapped and she melted against him, trapped by her own emotions.

She experienced a floating sensation, but when the springs of her bed creaked beneath their combined weight she knew what had happened, and panic acted like a douche of iced water, dousing the fires of her emotions. Jordan had discarded his jacket, and her frightened eyes were fastened on to the wide expanse of his tanned, hair-roughened chest where his shirt buttons had come undone.

'Let me go!' she begged hoarsely, but his hands were firm on her flesh, moulding, coaxing, driving away her fears until her trembling body was receptive, yielding, and aroused beyond reason.

'Oh, Margot, I want you,' he groaned against her breast, and she was hardly aware of what she was doing when she pushed her fingers through his dark, springy hair to hold his head against her while she savoured the sensually arousing touch of his lips on her responsive flesh.

'Jordan . . . this is wrong,' she moaned at last when a tiny thread of sanity wound its way to the surface of her mind, but his mouth found hers, and her conscience was smothered as the fire of his passion consumed her.

The persistent ringing of the telephone finally penetrated her drugged senses, and although Jordan murmured urgently that she should ignore it, she somehow managed to extricate herself from his arms to zip herself into her housecoat. Flushed and ashamed of herself, she stormed into the passage to answer the telephone, and the caller did not need to identify herself, for that autocratic voice could belong to none other than Eva Merrick.

'Would you please tell Jordan that Berdine has arrived?'

'Certainly,' Margot replied, a little startled, then the line went dead, and she replaced the receiver with a hand that was shaking visibly. 'That was your mother,' she told Jordan when she had brushed the hair out of her eyes to see him coming down the passage towards her. 'Berdine Powell has arrived, and I suggest that you don't keep her waiting.'

He pulled on his jacket and pushed agitated fingers

through his hair. 'Margot . . .'

'Please, Jordan,' she begged, stepping beyond the reach of his hands and too ashamed to meet his eyes. 'What happened just now was regrettable, but we might have regretted it a great deal more had the telephone not interrupted, and I must beg you not to read too much into my shameful behaviour. I'm totally inexperienced in this sort of thing, and if I've given you any encouragement in the past, then I assure you it's been unintentional, and I hope you'll forgive me.'

A brief, agonising silence followed this disclosure, then he snapped, 'Get to the point!'

Taking a deep, steadying breath, she said what she knew Eva Merrick expected of her. 'I don't want you to come here again, and I would prefer it if we don't meet socially in future unless it's absolutely unavoidable.'

'Are you perfectly sure that's what you want?'

'Perfectly,' she said, the calmness in her voice belying the aching turmoil within her. 'Go now . . . please. Your fiancée is waiting for you.'

'My . . . fiancée?' he questioned harshly, and she felt, rather than saw his eyes boring into her before she summoned up enough courage to throw back her head in order to look up at him.

'Yes,' she whispered huskily, forcing herself to smile. 'I know about your impending engagement to Berdine Powell, but you can rest assured that I shan't breathe a word of it to anyone until you yourself decide to make it public.'

His eyes glittered strangely, then narrowed. 'That's very considerate of you.'

He did not insult her intelligence with a denial, nor did he offer an explanation, and she supposed, cynically, that she ought to be grateful for this.

'Then you agree with me, Jordan, that it would be wiser for you not to come here again?'

'Oh, I agree absolutely,' he bit out the words, and his cold, expressionless face swam before her eyes long after he had slammed out of the house.

Margot leaned against the wall and closed her eyes. She felt drained and numb, and terribly, terribly empty, but deep down inside her a pain uncurled for which there was no known remedy, and with it came the agonising knowledge that she had been considered good enough only for a possible affair, while someone else would bear his name and his children.

# CHAPTER SIX

THE cool antipathy between the Theatre Sister and the Senior Surgeon did not go unnoticed during the days that followed, and Dr Neil Harris was the first to mention the subject during one lunch hour when he brought his cup of coffee over to Margot's table and sat down without waiting for an invitation.

'What's up between Merrick and yourself?' he asked bluntly. 'The atmosphere is anything but convivial in the theatre these days.' When Margot did not reply he eyed her quizzically over the rim of his cup. 'Has the arrival of a certain blonde lady anything to do with it?'

'So she's blonde, is she?' Margot thought cynically, but aloud, she said: 'I don't know what you're talking about.'

'Oh, come now, Margot,' Neil Harris laughed. 'You must have heard the rumour that Jordan's going to marry the lovely Berdine Powell, whom he met, by the way, on the ski slopes while they were holidaying in Switzerland.'

Margot did not care very much where they met each other; not when jealousy flowed like a swift, searing fire through her veins, but she concealed her feelings admirably, and faced the man seated opposite her without a flicker of emotion crossing her lovely face. 'I don't pay much attention to rumours.'

'This isn't just a rumour, sweetheart, it's fact.'

'What Dr Merrick chooses to do with his personal

life is no concern of mine.'

'You saw quite a lot of each other recently, though,' he remarked with a speculative gleam in his eyes.

'Dr Merrick was kind to me when my mother died, and . . .' Her throat tightened at the memory, and she swallowed to disperse with the constriction to add hastily '. . . That was all.'

'Pity,' Neil Harris sighed a little dramatically. 'I was beginning to think there was a secret romance going on under our very noses.'

'You were mistaken,' Margot smiled frozenly. 'You said yourself that he's going to marry Berdine Powell.'

'There's many a slip 'twixt cup and lip, if you'll forgive me quoting that old adage,' he remarked, 'and it's all still in the rumour stage, of course.'

Margot pushed aside her empty cup and rose to her feet. 'I think it's time we returned to the theatre. Dr Grant is operating, and he hates being kept waiting.'

Neil Harris swallowed down the remainder of his coffee and followed her reluctantly. He could not argue that the Chief was a demon when there was just the slightest disruption in the planned schedule.

At Joanne's invitation Margot spent the Sunday at their home and, as asked, she brought her tennis gear along. There were several guests other than herself, she discovered, and Jordan, his mother, and Berdine Powell were among them. Tall, blonde and shapely, Berdine had an attractive Nordic appearance about her, but after a closer look Margot began to suspect that she also possessed some of that region's iciness in her veins.

Margot felt a little lost, at first, until she was introduced to Joanne's brother, Bruce Webster, who had come to stay for a few weeks. Tall, lean and fair, he could not have been more than a year older than

Margot, but there was an instant rapport between them which diminished a great deal of Margot's awkwardness at finding herself faced with Jordan, his fiancée, and the glaring disapproval in Eva Merrick's eyes whenever their glances met.

It was a hot September day and Joanne served a cold lunch out on the wide terrace of her home. Everyone, except Jordan's mother, seemed to be in a jovial, carefree mood as they helped themselves to cold turkey, mutton and salads before going in search of a chair in a shady spot to escape the piercing rays of the mid-day sun.

With Bruce at her side Margot felt oddly protected, and when he suggested a game of tennis later that afternoon, she agreed readily.

'I'm not very good at it, though,' she warned, her generous mouth curved in a rueful smile.

'Neither am I,' Bruce grimaced. 'Squash is really my game, but I enjoy a leisurely game of tennis once in a while.'

They went inside to change, and some minutes later Margot was sweating it out on the tennis court, using all her powers of concentration, and the little knowledge she possessed, to return Bruce's slashing services, but her efforts were rewarded when he beat her only by a very narrow margin.

'You play quite a strong game of tennis,' he complimented her while he towelled the perspiration from his tanned face.

'And you play a far better game than you led me to believe,' she laughed accusingly.

'I'll let you win next time,' he grinned when they seated themselves on a wooden bench beneath the shady oak, and her ready smile flashed out for the first time in weeks.

'Is that what you call chauvinistic condescension?' she questioned humorously.

He shook his damp, fair head, and grinned wickedly once more. 'I call it gentlemanly politeness,' he contradicted her.

Margot ceased dabbing at her own hot face and took a playful swipe at Bruce with her towel before she sat down beside him to regain her breath, and drink in the peace of her surroundings, but her peace was shortlived when she caught sight of Jordan and Berdine approaching them across the lawn.

Compared to Margot, who felt hot and sticky after her game, Berdine looked cool and elegant somehow in her short tennis dress, but it was Jordan who captured and held Margot's heart-stopping attention. 'Such a nice boy,' her mother had once labelled him, but there was nothing boyish about those long, muscular legs, and the lean hips clad in white tennis shorts. The white silk shirt seemed a fraction too tight to accommodate the width of his powerful shoulders, and even in this unusual attire his virile masculinity was potently evident to Margot, who felt that familiar weakness invading her limbs as she recalled vividly those moments when the hard length of his body had lain so close against her own during those last mad moments they had shared together.

Jordan's dark eyes flicked impersonally over Margot, and it was to Bruce that he addressed himself. 'Would the two of you care for a game of doubles?'

'We wouldn't mind at all,' Bruce replied before Margot's paralysed tongue could be forced into action.

They spun for partners as well as for service and, with Margot's rotten luck, she found herself partnering

Jordan. Among all his many accomplishments at school Jordan had been an excellent tennis player, Margot recalled unwillingly, and, as they plunged into the game, she noticed that he had lost none of his tenacity on the court. Inspired rather than deflated, she played the best game she had ever played before, and, after a gruelling hour of thrashing the ball about, Bruce and Berdine were forced to admit defeat.

'Thanks, partner,' Jordan smiled faintly as he turned to Margot, and her hand was engulfed in his for a brief moment before the others joined them.

'Poor thing,' Berdine purred up at Jordan, and Margot could not help noticing that she still looked remarkably fresh after their tiring match. 'You must be exhausted after having to take us on almost single-handed,' Berdine continued, sliding her arm possessively through Jordan's.

'Nonsense!' he laughed shortly. 'Margot played an excellent game of tennis, and you're forgetting, perhaps, that we came on to the court fresh while Bruce and Margot had already been tired out after their first match.'

Margot's heart leapt at the compliment, but it subsided swiftly when she encountered Berdine's cool, calculating glance resting on her for a brief moment before those pale grey eyes focussed themselves once more on Jordan.

'You're right, of course, darling,' she pouted prettily, 'but then you always are, aren't you?'

'Anyone for a cool orange drink?' Joanne interrupted lightly, arriving at the right moment to prevent the situation from developing into something awkward and tense.

'Yes, please,' they chorussed, and Joanne placed the

tray on the slatted wooden table to pour the iced orange juice into the tall glasses.

Seated between Bruce and Joanne, Margot experienced the odd sensation that she was being protected from something unpleasant; shielded, in fact, from the disturbing quality of Jordan's penetrating, dark glances, and Berdine's shrewd, prolonged stares.

'I can't stand that woman,' Joanne remarked with surprising fierceness when Jordan and Berdine finally excused themselves to rejoin his mother on the terrace. 'Berdine reminds me of a sticky honey jar,' she added with a distasteful grimace.

'Now, now, Jo, don't be catty,' Bruce warned humorously.

'I'm not being catty,' Joanne responded vehemently. 'I'm merely speaking my mind, and I can't for the life of me understand how a man of Jordan's intelligence could tolerate the cloying manner of a woman who's nothing but an empty vessel.'

Bruce's grey eyes gleamed wickedly. 'Maybe he's partial to sticky honey jars?'

'I somehow don't imagine he is,' Joanne returned swiftly, turning to frown at her brother. 'If you ask me, his mother is behind this entire set-up.'

At this point Margot felt the need to intervene, and she did so with surprising calmness. 'Jordan isn't the sort of man who would allow himself to be manipulated by anyone, not even by his mother, and if Mrs Merrick has had anything to do with this, then Jordan must have given it his approval.'

Brother and sister exchanged glances during the peculiar little silence that followed Margot's statement, then Joanne turned to Margot and asked with frowning solemnity, 'Tell me, Margot, can you honestly see

Jordan happily married to that—that *woman*?'

'She's beautiful and sophisticated, and she has just the right sort of background to be welcomed into the Merrick fold,' Margot responded without hesitation, but each word drove the sword deeper into her own wounded heart.

'Background!' Joanne snorted indignantly. 'One doesn't need background to have breeding, and you have far more of the latter in your little finger than Berdine Powell will ever have in her entire anatomy, and that's a fact!'

Having delivered her forceful little speech, Joanne picked up the tray and marched off towards the house, leaving Bruce and Margot alone under the shady oak.

'I can tell the way my sister's mind is working,' Bruce remarked humorously, and Margot's startled eyes met his as he added: 'She considers you would make Jordan an excellent wife.'

'She's wrong. I wouldn't,' Margot replied with that cool defensiveness behind which she was forced to hide her true feelings. 'I don't come from the right side of town in the first place . . .'

'That's utter nonsense!' Bruce interjected sharply.

'. . . and in the second place, I'm not making myself available as a candidate,' she continued as if he had not spoken.

'But you'd like to.'

The words were quietly spoken, but they were delivered with a shocking clarity that penetrated her self-control, and she heard herself say thickly, 'You're mistaken.'

'Am I?'

She lowered her lashes swiftly, but when she raised them a few moments later he saw the glimmer of moisture in her eyes, and the slight quivering of her lips when she smiled a little whimsically and whispered, 'You're much too shrewd, Bruce.'

'I grew up the hard way, and so did Joanne,' he smiled, covering her hands in her lap with one of his own. 'And if there's one thing we've learnt, then it's this: if you want something badly enough, you'll go all out to get it. I'm not saying one must trample on others in the process, but it's what you make of yourself that counts and, with Daniel's help, both Joanne and I succeeded.'

'With Daniel's help?' she queried confusedly, forgetting for a moment her own problems.

'I suppose you know that Jo and I were left pretty destitute after our parents died,' Bruce began his explanation. 'Our uncle took us in, much against his wife's wishes, and paid for our education. Joanne went into nursing, and I finally studied engineering at varsity. My uncle provided the funds, with the understanding that Joanne and I would pay him back as soon as I'd qualified, and then he died suddenly, and unexpectedly. He'd made no provision for this agreement in his will, and his wife promptly stopped the monthly payments into my account.'

'Is this where Daniel comes in?' Margot risked asking.

'Yes,' he nodded, removing his hand from hers to light a cigarette. 'At Daniel's suggestion Joanne married him to satisfy his dying mother's whim to see him settled in marriage, and in return for Jo's acceptance he paid my university fees.' He blew a cloud of agitated smoke into the afternoon air. 'I never knew this at the time, of course, or I would never have agreed to Joanne sacrificing herself in this manner for my sake alone.

Everything seemed to be quite normal between them while Daniel's mother was still alive, but after her death things went wrong. Daniel went off to Switzerland for a year, and Joanne accepted a post here in Willowmead, but in the end everything worked out happily for them.'

Margot understood now what a shock it must have been for Joanne when Daniel arrived so unexpectedly in Willowmead, and she understood, too, why their marriage had been kept such a secret until they had had time to sort out their differences.

'Did everything work out happily for you too?' she asked at length.

'It certainly did,' Bruce nodded. 'I can't tell you how much I appreciate what Daniel did for me, and I'm repaying my loan with a smile.'

'I can't believe that they married each other for those cold-blooded reasons alone,' she mused aloud. 'I've seen them together, and I've seen the way they look at each other when they think no one is watching.'

'Oh, they married each other for all the wrong reasons, but they loved each other all the same. They were just a little slow in admitting it,' Bruce laughed, then he sobered and faced Margot directly. 'You're in love with Jordan, aren't you.'

It was a statement, not a question, but even in this moment of absolute honesty between Bruce and herself she could not admit that he was correct in his assumption, and she laughed a little shakily as she explained.

'I met Jordan for the first time when I was ten years old and he a lordly eighteen, and for six years he was my hero, my idol, and all the silly things little girls dream of.'

'What happened then?'

'His pedestal collapsed, and he became a mortal with

feet of clay when I discovered that he was a status-conscious snob just like his mother.' Her expression hardened unconsciously as she added through her clenched teeth, 'I despised him for it.'

'He spent seven years in Europe, I believe.'

'Yes,' she nodded absently, 'and when he came back . . .'

'You found that you didn't despise him as much as you thought you did,' he finished for her shrewdly when she paused, and Margot shook herself free of the emotions which tightened her throat and filled her eyes with that familiar, damp warmth.

'Let's change the subject,' she said abruptly.

'Will you have dinner with me one evening?' he obliged willingly.

'I'd like that very much,' she smiled up at him, in complete control of herself once more.

'I'll give you a ring some time to arrange the time and the place,' Bruce promised and, picking up their tennis racquets, they strolled back to the house.

'I'd like to see the operating schedule for tomorrow,' said Jordan when he walked into Margot's office late on the Monday afternoon.

'Certainly, Dr Merrick,' she replied, rising respectfully to her feet and passing him the schedule he required, but as she did so the telephone on her desk rang shrilly and, muttering an apology, she lifted the receiver to hear a now familiar voice addressing her.

'Bruce, how lovely to hear from you!' she could not help exclaiming, and neither could she help noticing the way Jordan's eyebrows shot upwards in a mocking curve.

'What about having dinner with me tomorrow evening?' Bruce's voice interrupted her observations.

'Yes, I'd like that,' she said at once, only too aware that Jordan was listening to every word she was saying. 'What time?'

'I'll pick you up at seven, if that's all right with you.'

'That would suit me perfectly,' she agreed without hesitation.

'See you tomorrow, then.'

'I presume that was Bruce Webster?' Jordan queried with a hint of disapproval in the set of his hard jaw.

'You presume correctly,' she replied with her head held high at an angle of defiance, but her defiance turned to anger at his next remark.

'He's too young for you.'

'I happen to like his company, and I don't see that it's any business of yours, Dr Merrick, if you'll forgive me saying so.'

'Since when have you needed my permission to speak your mind?'

His cynical smile merely fanned her anger and, relying heavily on every scrap of self-control she possessed, she said calmly, 'If you've finished with that schedule, Dr Merrick, I hope you'll excuse me. I have to bring this log book up to date before I can think of going home.'

Sparks of anger glittered in his eyes as he flicked the schedule on to the log book and leaned towards her across the desk. 'I hope you realise, Margot, that what's happened between us is of your own making.'

She stared at the unrelenting line of his square jaw, and the twist of cruelty on the mouth which she had found so sensually persuasive against her own at times. But this was not the time nor the place for those kind of thoughts, she told herself fiercely, then she heard herself asking with surprising coldness, 'Are you blaming me, Dr Merrick, for your callous, inconsiderate behaviour?'

'Callous and inconsiderate?' he barked at her, his nostrils flaring with barely controlled anger. 'In what way, if I may know, was I callous and inconsiderate towards you?'

'You certainly don't need me to enlighten you,' she stated flatly, turning away from his tempting nearness, and the undeniable longing to be held in arms which were not meant for her, but Jordan was not going to let her get away with it as easily as that.

A heavy hand came down on to her shoulder and she was spun round roughly to encounter the taunting, stabbing mockery of those narrowed dark eyes.

'As I recall, I made love to you a little,' he enunciated smoothly, 'but there was nothing callous or inconsiderate about it. *And*, if I remember correctly, you enjoyed every moment of it as much as I did.'

'Need you remind me of that?' she hissed up at him, his nearness stirring her senses to the point of madness. 'Haven't I been humiliated enough?'

'It was never my intention to humiliate you, Margot.'

'Perhaps not,' she agreed, her voice raw with pride and hurt anger. 'But you can't deny that you were seeking a cheap thrill at my expense.'

His bone-crushing grip on her shoulder increased, and she bit down hard on her lip to prevent herself from crying out.

'Watch what you're saying, Margot,' he warned with ominous softness. 'I might just forget where we are and teach you a lesson you're not likely to forget in a hurry.'

Interminable, frightening seconds seemed to pass before she lowered her eyes and drew a careful breath.

'With respect, Dr Merrick,' she managed somehow, 'this is my office, and will you kindly leave it.'

She felt the anger in his touch, and thought for a moment that he would do her a physical injury, but he released her abruptly and swung about on his heel to leave her alone in the small, clinical office with her heart pounding, her palms damp, and her mouth curiously dry.

Margot sat down heavily in her chair and a tiredness she had never known before seemed to swamp her body. These altercations between Jordan and herself did not exactly make life easier for her in her work, and neither was she happy at home. The silent emptiness of the house brought on a feeling of acute loneliness; a loneliness she had never known before, and it was during those long, dark hours of the night that she realised how much she missed her mother. It was then, too, that she longed achingly for Jordan's presence, his touch, and the forbidden rapture of his kisses, but her arms remained empty, and her pillow was damp each morning when she dragged herself out of bed to face another day.

What was the point of brooding over these painful moments in her life? she wondered tiredly as she drew the log book closer and made the last few entries for the day before draping her cape about her shoulders and picking up her handbag. She was tired, she decided when she walked out of her office and closed the door behind her. Her self-control was always at its lowest ebb at this time of day, and all she wanted at that moment was to go home to her bed, to sleep, if possible, and to forget.

When Margot awoke the following morning she felt thick-headed and tight-chested, but, after swallowing down a couple of tablets as a precautionary measure against influenza, she forgot about it for the rest of the day. It was not until she was dressing for her dinner appointment with Bruce Webster that evening that she felt again that slight thickness in her head and that peculiar tightness in her chest. She took a couple of aspirins once again, and after a few moments she experienced a measure of relief which made her forget about her physical discomfort for the next few hours.

At the motel, later that evening, Margot tried desperately to thrust aside the memory of the evening she had dined there with Jordan. She longed to spend a quiet and restful evening with Bruce, but her hopes were shattered shortly after their arrival.

Jordan and Berdine were seated at a table across the candlelit room, and Margot's heart almost stopped functioning when she first looked up to find those dark eyes surveying her so intently across the space dividing them. For some ridiculous reason she felt like a child caught in the act of doing something wrong, and she wrenched her eyes from his when an angry and embarrassed flush stained her cheeks.

Margot had hardly had time to compose herself when the head waiter approached their table carrying a folded note on a silver tray, and Bruce read through the written message swiftly before passing it on to Margot with a query in his eyes.

Jordan's strong, decisive handwriting leapt out at her from the small sheet of white paper. *'Would you care to join us and make a foursome for dinner? J.M.'*

'Do you have a pen handy, by any chance?' Margot asked Bruce, making a snap decision as she did so, and when he passed his pen across the table towards her she wrote a hasty reply on the same sheet of paper before

handing it to the waiter who had stood waiting discreetly beside the table.

*'Thank you, but no,'* she wrote back with some inso-
lence. *'We wouldn't want to spoil your evening, and ours.
M.H.'*

'Don't burn your boats, Margot,' Bruce warned
when he had glimpsed what she had written, and a wry
smile curved her generous mouth.

'Jordan has the authority to manipulate my life at the
clinic, but my private life is my own, and I alone have
the right to choose whom I shall spend my time with,'
she explained tritely.

The meal Bruce had ordered arrived shortly afterwards, but Margot could just as well have been eating
sawdust. She had a dreadful feeling that her indisposi-
tion was not entirely due to the menacing glances
Jordan shot in their direction from time to time across
the heads of the other diners, and neither did she think
it had anything to do with the food itself. The expertise
of the motel's chef was undoubtedly to be complimented, but Margot was incapable of doing justice to
the superb dishes.

'I have the distinct feeling that we're being glared at,'
Bruce remarked shrewdly when they finally sampled the
sweet.

Margot smiled at him with a certain devilment lurking in her eyes and tingling in her veins. 'I have that
same feeling, but I don't mind. Do you?'

'No,' Bruce shook his fair head and grinned, moving
his shoulders beneath the immaculate fit of his jacket.
'Just as long as my suit doesn't catch fire while I'm still
in it!'

Margot laughed at that, but when her surreptitious
glance met those dark eyes across the room she felt a

little ashamed of her behaviour.

'Thank you, Bruce. That was a superb dinner,' she smiled untruthfully when, at last, they had finished off their meal with a cup of aromatic coffee.

'Shall we go through to the lounge?' he suggested as they rose from the table, and when she nodded he placed her wrap about her shoulders. 'They've cleared a space for dancing in the room adjoining the lounge,' he added enthusiastically.

Margot did not feel very much like dancing, but she agreed nevertheless, not wanting to spoil the evening for her companion. A few moments later, though, she wished fervently that she *had* refused, for Jordan and Berdine had somehow reached the lounge before them, and Jordan was advancing upon them in a manner which suggested that he was determined not to be thwarted a second time.

'Ah, Bruce! This is quite an occasion,' said Jordan, placing a restraining hand on the younger man's shoulder. 'You'll join us for a drink, I'm sure.'

'Well, I——' Bruce hesitated and glanced with a certain amount of uncertainty at Margot, who had gone still beside him, but the next instant Jordan had placed himself between them and was ushering them towards the corner table where Berdine sat waiting with a curiously bored expression on her lovely Nordic features.

'Waiter?' Jordan clicked his fingers the moment they were seated. 'Champagne, please, and I want a bottle of the best you have.'

The Malay bowed respectfully and disappeared into the back, and only then did Berdine stir herself to smile with melting sweetness at the man seated close to her.

'Jordan darling, you're being deliciously extravagant,

but we did promise your mother we would be home early, didn't we?'

'I made no such promise at all,' Jordan contradicted with surprising abruptness. 'The night is still young, and Mother is quite capable of taking care of herself.'

'If you say so, darling,' Berdine pouted, 'but she did look rather peckish when we left the house this evening.'

'She was sulking, my dear Berdine,' Jordan smiled faintly, but there was a hard, relentless glitter in the depths of his eyes as he faced the beautiful woman beside him. 'I've known my mother long enough to realise that she can't stand not being allowed to manipulate my life.' A shadow fell across the table, and he looked up sharply. 'Ah, the champagne.'

Margot felt that now familiar dryness rise from her tight chest into her throat as she watched Jordan pour the champagne into delicately stemmed glasses, and she could not help thinking that if she had wanted proof that his association with Berdine was entirely of his own making, then she had received it, and the discovery left a taste of bitterness in her mouth.

'Here's to the rest of the evening,' Jordan said at last, his glance going from one to the other as he raised his glass. 'May it blossom into something fruitful.'

Margot raised her glass to her lips, but, when her eyes met Jordan's for one brief second, she felt a cold little shiver travelling up her spine, and wondered why she should have had the peculiar notion that his toast had hidden a veiled threat to her. She must surely be mistaken, she decided, but her back was aching with rigidness, and her trembling fingers tightened about the stem of her glass when she raised it to her lips to sip at the sparkling liquid.

# CHAPTER SEVEN

MARGOT was certain that she had never felt more miserable in her entire life as she watched Jordan circling the floor with the beautiful Berdine in his arms, and she had to admit, albeit reluctantly, that they complemented each other in every way, most especially since Jordan was so dark, and Berdine so fair. She looked magnificent, too, Margot thought, in that black, flowing evening gown with its off-the-shoulder neckline that exposed the superb smoothness of that perfect neck and shoulders.

'Bruce, is there any reason why we should stay longer?' Margot wanted to know when he finally persuaded her on to the dance floor. 'Couldn't we just disappear quietly without anyone noticing?'

Bruce grinned down at her. 'You could plead a headache, I suppose, but I don't somehow think the good doctor would swallow that old worn-out excuse.'

'No, I don't suppose he would,' she agreed with a grimace, then she added with a certain vehemence, 'Oh, how I *hate* that man!'

'I know,' Bruce murmured against her ear. 'It's terrible to hate someone like that.'

She drew back a little to glance up at him suspiciously. 'Are you making fun of me, Bruce?'

'I've never been more serious,' he assured her without a flicker of a smile crossing his lean features. 'Love and hate are two equally painful emotions, I'm told, but indifference is an emotion I should imagine one could cope with quite comfortably.'

'Indifference,' she murmured, sampling the word on her tongue and wincing inwardly. 'I don't think anyone could be entirely indifferent to Jordan. One would either love him, or hate him, and . . .'

'And you love him,' he concluded when she paused selfconsciously.

'Stop saying that!'

'It's true, though,' Bruce persisted, tightening his arm about her waist when she tried to escape from him, and she was forced to listen to the rest of what he had to say. 'it's there in your eyes whenever you look at him, and you can't deny it,' he stated firmly.

'Oh, God!' She stilled in his arms, her steps faltering momentarily while they danced. 'Am I making myself so obvious?'

'Not to him, I don't imagine, but to an outsider like myself it's pretty obvious where your heart lies, and the lovely Berdine is beginning to suspect as well, if I'm not mistaken.'

'Lord! I shall have to watch my step if I don't want——' Margot broke off abruptly and laughed a little selfconsciously. 'Now I've given myself away completely, haven't I?'

'I'm afraid so,' Bruce grinned down at her wickedly, then he took her arm and ushered her back to the table. 'I think we can both do with a drink.'

Later, when Margot found herself seated opposite Berdine, she had to admit to herself that Bruce had assumed correctly. The woman Jordan intended to marry was eyeing her with more than just ordinary curiosity, and on several occasions, when Jordan had chosen to pay attention to Margot, Berdine's pale grey eyes had flashed with unmistakable malice in Margot's direction. She would have to take care, and a great deal more care than she had taken in the past, Margot warned herself.

'This one is mine, I think,' Jordan announced, rising and extending his hand towards Margot when the band started playing a slow waltz, and for one paralysing moment she felt incapable of movement, then she placed her hand in his and allowed him to draw her to her feet, conscious of Bruce's quizzical glance and Berdine's cold, speculative stare.

'I'm not very good at dancing,' she warned nervously, but he made no comment as he drew her into his arms.

His hand was warm against the hollow of her back, guiding her so that her steps matched his perfectly, but she drew back sharply moments later when he tried to draw her closer.

'Relax, Margot,' he growled down at her. 'I merely want to dance with you, not make love to you.'

'No one else but you would have the gall to say something like that,' she flashed up at him angrily.

'Be quiet!' His lowered voice had the effect of a whiplash and she paled visibly, but she found herself obeying, somehow, and relaxing to the extent that she allowed him to draw her closer until their bodies touched, sparking off that current of sensual awareness while they moved in rhythmic unison to the music. She came very close to losing herself completely in the magic of the moment, but the spell was broken when he whispered warmly in her ear, 'You're beautiful this evening, Margot. More beautiful than I've ever seen you before.'

Under different circumstances his compliment might have made her glow with an inner happiness, but at that moment it had the effect of a splash of iced water, jerking her rapidly to her senses.

'You said that to Berdine as well, I'm sure,' she replied sarcastically, drawing a little away from the disturbing closeness of his body.

'Berdine never needs to be told that she's beautiful,' he said at once, the hard line of his jaw growing taut. 'She's well aware of her physical attractions, and she knows just how to exploit each one of them to their best advantage.'

'She not only looks it, but she also sounds as if she would suit you admirably,' Margot remarked coldly, despising herself for the hint of jealousy she detected in her voice.

'Now that you come to mention it, yes. She suits me admirably,' he admitted, thrusting that painful sword deep into her very soul. 'She's not plagued by prejudices, and fanciful, misguided notions.'

'Such as I am, I suppose,' she could not help saying, but she wished desperately that she could retract those words the second they were uttered, and she wished it most especially when she saw that coldly mocking smile lurk about his mouth.

'You said it, Margot. Remember that!'

'I think I've had enough, if you don't mind,' she said at last, the dull throbbing against her temples giving her the legitimate excuse to add: 'I have a headache.'

'Fresh air is what you need,' Jordan concluded at once, and before she could utter a word of protest she was being steered through the dancing couples on the floor and out on to the terrace where the cool mountain air brushed soothingly against her hot cheeks and pounding temples, but she struggled against the forceful grip of those clever hands when he drew her deeper into the shadows.

'Oh, please, I don't think there's any need for——'

'Goodness' sake, Margot!' He swung her forcibly into the shadows and gripped her shoulders so hard that she almost cried out. 'I think, of all the women I've ever known, you're the most infuriating!'

'Must you conquer every female who crosses your line of vision?' she demanded, her breath coming fast over parted lips as she felt those hard thighs brush against her own.

'Don't make me angry, Margot. You know there's no truth in your statement, but I'd like to know what I've done to deserve your absurd opinions, and your hatred?'

'I—I don't hate you,' she stammered helplessly.

'There are times when you behave as if you do, and I would like to know why.'

'The answer lies with you.'

'If there's one thing I can't tolerate, then it's a riddle, so let's have the truth without the trimmings,' Jordan demanded, his eyes glittering oddly in the moonlight, and his hands no longer punishing as they moved with sensual slowness down her back, filling her with a desperate longing to surrender to the mad desire to press closer to him.

His warm breath stirred the silky hair against her temples before travelling across her cheek to her mouth, but she came to her senses when his lips descended to take what she had been offering so unconsciously, and she turned her flushed face away, avoiding his lips to say unsteadily, 'Please, Jordan, it's been a long day, I'm tired, and I'd like Bruce to take me home.'

'Dammit, Margot, you owe me an explanation!' he ground out the words, and when his hands tightened like a vice about her slender waist she raised wide, imploring eyes to his.

He ignored her silent plea, and his head descended until the hard, bruising quality of his mouth against her own brought tears to her eyes, but, before she could respond, the rustle of silk made them draw apart, and seconds later a lilting voice remarked rather petulantly,

'Darling, we've been worried simply out of our minds, haven't we, Bruce?'

In her sick, bewildered state, Margot could not help noticing that Bruce did not have the appearance of someone who had spent a few worrying moments alone. He seemed annoyed, in fact, at having been dragged along to become involved in Berdine's intervention, and he also looked decidedly uncomfortable standing there next to that Nordic beauty.

'Margot developed a headache from the stuffiness inside, so I brought her out for a breath of fresh air,' Jordan explained with admirable calmness before Margot could find her voice, and beneath Berdine's sweet look of concern she sensed a glimmer of malice.

'What a shame,' Berdine remarked with a solicitude that did not ring true. 'You do look rather flushed.'

'She knows,' Margot thought. 'She knows damn well that my flushed appearance has nothing to do with a headache.'

'I'm sorry, Bruce,' Margot apologised, recovering her composure and deciding that she had endured enough embarrassment for one night. 'Will you take me home now, please?'

Bruce nodded and, ignoring Berdine, said: 'Excuse us, Jordan, will you?'

Margot somehow found herself being escorted inside, across the section of the dance floor where couples still swayed in tune to the music, and through the wide arch into the lounge beyond. Her wrap was placed about her shivering form, and Bruce's arm was like a fortress that was draped comfortably about her as he took her out to where he had parked his car. Neither of them spoke a word until, twenty minutes later, they walked up the path to her front door.

'What happened, Margot?' Bruce asked quietly.

'Nothing unusual,' she sighed, fighting against the peculiar exhaustion which had her in its grip. 'Whenever Jordan and I got together the sparks seem to fly, and we're almost literally at each other's throats.'

Bruce smiled that twisted smile of his which she had come to know so well in the short space of time they had known each other, then he said jokingly, 'That's what you call an explosive chemical reaction.'

'I don't very much care what you call it, but it always hurts like hell afterwards,' she replied, attempting to match his humorous expression, but not quite succeeding.

'If you need a shoulder to cry on . . .'

'I'll call you,' she promised tiredly, 'and thank you for being such an understanding companion.'

'That's what friends are for, not so?'

His lips brushed against her cheek in a brotherly fashion, and then he was gone, leaving her alone with her throbbing headache and a tiredness which seemed to be finding its way into the very marrow of her bones.

Margot's headache did not ease off by morning, and she swallowed down a couple more aspirins when she got up to make herself a cup of coffee, but she realised soon afterwards that she would be incapable of coping with the long hours in the operating theatre that day. She was hot and flushed, and would probably be better off in bed, she told herself sensibly as she staggered a little drunkenly towards the telephone to notify the clinic that she would not be reporting for duty that morning.

After making the necessary telephone call she crawled back into bed, too exhausted to do anything but sleep feverishly and fitfully until late that afternoon when a shaking chill was followed up by a stabbing pain in her chest. She realised then that she was not suffering from an ordinary bout of influenza. Her symptoms were definitely more than that, and the sooner she contacted Dr Turner, the better for her, but her limbs felt as heavy as lead, and she knew, with a sinking feeling of utter helplessness, that she would never reach the telephone if she were left to her own devices.

She tried to lever herself up out of bed, but her efforts were so weak and futile that she started to cry and ended up coughing, each cough tearing away at her chest until it felt as if she were on fire with the agony of it. She reached for the glass of water beside her bed, but in her clumsy state she knocked it over. This brought on a fresh bout of tears which resulted in a coughing fit that lasted until, hot and ill, she sank into a restless oblivion where her feverish disposition no longer seemed to matter to her.

'Margot!' a deep, familiar voice finally succeeded in penetrating her dulled senses. 'Margot, can you hear me?'

'Oh, no!' she croaked a little hysterically when her feverish eyes fastened on to Jordan's distorted features. 'Of all people, it had to be you!'

'I know,' he agreed soberly, looking oddly white as he covered her with an extra blanket, and sponged her hot face with a cool, damp cloth. 'I always seem to arrive at the wrong place at the right time, don't I?' he added, but he sounded totally unamused, and she wondered vaguely why this should be so.

'How—how did you get in?'

'The kitchen door was unlocked,' he replied shortly. 'Now shut up, will you, there's a good girl.'

When Margot came to her senses a second time she was lying in an unfamiliar room with high white walls surrounding her. She was in an uncomfortable bed with railings on both sides of her, but Jordan was still there, his presence so familiar and so comforting that she wanted to cry when his cool hands soothed her brow.

'Where—Where am I?' she croaked in a voice that did not sound at all like her own.

'You're in hospital.'

'Oh, no!' she moaned, hot tears spilling over on to her cheeks before she could prevent them and, embarrassed, she turned her face away towards the opposite wall just as oblivion claimed her once more.

She recalled very little of those first few days in hospital, but she knew that she had surfaced on a few occasions to find herself encased in an oxygen tent. It had frightened her at first, but she had appreciated it afterwards when she discovered that she no longer had to struggle for air, or fight against the burning, suffocating pressure in her chest.

It was several days, however, before Dr Turner allowed her to have visitors, and her first visitor was an anxious-looking Joanne Grant.

'We've all been so terribly worried about you, Margot,' she said, her green glance registering concern as it travelled over the pale, thin girl lying against the pillows with dark smudges beneath her sunken eyes. 'How are you feeling today?'

'Tired, but reasonably well, thank you,' Margot managed in a whisper, then she frowned in concentration. 'I—I think Jordan was here. Was it—was it my imagination?'

'It wasn't your imagination. Jordan cancelled all his scheduled operations to be here with you until the crisis was over,' Joanne explained, and a smile curved her mouth when she noticed the look of incredulity stealing into Margot's blue, lifeless eyes.

'I have an idea that he brought me here, but I——' Margot swallowed convulsively and blinked rapidly to hold back the tears which seemed to hover so perilously close to the surface, then she shook her head dumbly until she could trust her voice sufficiently to say, 'No, I didn't know that he spent so much time here with—with me.'

'He was most concerned about you.'

'Was he?' Margot asked with sudden cynicism. 'I bet his mother and Berdine were not too happy about that.'

'Who cares?' Joanne laughed, then, with a quick glance at her wristwatch, she said: 'I can't stay long, but you must realise that your convalescence is going to be long and slow.'

'Yes, I know,' Margot sighed, and not feeling strong enough yet to give it much thought.

'When you're fit enough to leave here you're coming home with me. Is that understood?'

'Joanne ... you have Serena, your husband, your home.' Margot shook her head tiredly, and closed her eyes for a brief moment before she once again met Joanne's steady gaze. 'You couldn't possibly take on this added responsibility.'

'Rubbish!' Joanne exclaimed, and a look of grim determination settled on her lovely face. 'You're coming home with me, and that's final,' she insisted.

A smile quivered on Margot's lips. 'Do you always have your own way with everything?'

'Not always, and not with everything. Daniel sees to that,' Joanne laughed, but she sobered again almost at once. 'You will do me the honour of being my guest, won't you?'

A lengthy silence lingered in the private ward during which a stern, white-clad figure indicated to Joanne that it was time to go, and only then did Margot whisper in a tired voice, 'Thank you, Joanne. I would like that very much.'

'Good!' Joanne pushed back her chair and stooped over Margot to kiss her lightly on the cheek. 'See you again tomorrow.'

Joanne and Bruce were regular visitors after that, but Dr Turner did not encourage Margot to see too many people until she was much stronger, and it was not until the day before she was to be allowed out of hospital that Jordan decided to honour her once again with his presence.

She was resting in a chair beside the window that afternoon when something told her she was no longer alone and, turning her head, she found Jordan observing her from across the room. He was immaculate, as always, in a suit of expensive grey cloth which was tailored superbly to fit his broad-shouldered, lean-hipped physique, but her heart behaved in the most irrational manner when her glance travelled upwards to encounter the intense scrutiny of those dark eyes.

'May I come in?' he asked with that familiar smile of mockery curving his hard yet sensuous mouth.

'You're in already, I notice,' she replied, hiding her feelings behind a wall of sarcasm.

His eyebrows rose sharply. 'Am I unwelcome?'

Margot stared at him now with a wariness she only now partially understood herself, and it stemmed from embarrassment, confusion, and a shyness she had believed she had outgrown. She still had no idea why he should have arrived at her home at that precise moment she had needed someone, and she had wondered frequently in what state of undress he had found her that night. She was afraid, too, of what she might have let slip during those moments of delirium of which she had no recollection and, added to this, she was puzzled by the knowledge that he had taken time off from the clinic to remain with her.

'If I said you were welcome,' she said at last, 'you'd misconstrue my meaning, and if I said the opposite you'd consider me an ungrateful wretch, so perhaps I'd better not answer your question at all.'

'Thanks for the invitation,' he bowed mockingly, drawing up a chair close to hers and seating himself with one long, muscular leg crossed over the other while he observed her through narrowed eyes. 'Your hospitality has always been beyond reproach,' he added bitingly, and it somehow brought her to her senses.

'I may be lacking in hospitality, but . . .' She swallowed convulsively and tried again. 'I *am* grateful, Jordan, for whatever reason brought you to my home that evening, and I'm grateful for everything you did for me afterwards.'

'So it's gratitude I'm receiving, is it?' he remarked with a harsh cynicism that placed her instantly on the defensive.

'You surely didn't expect more from me than that, did you?'

'From you?' he laughed harshly, and the sound

grated along her sensitive nerves until they vibrated uncomfortably. 'No, Margot,' he shook his dark head. 'There's nothing I want from you, and there's nothing you could give me that I don't already have.'

Stung by his words, she retaliated swiftly with, 'I never ever imagined anything to the contrary!'

'Then it seems to me we understand each other at last.'

'I think we understand each other perfectly, and we have done so for a long time.'

'Dammit, Margot!' he growled, breaking the brief, electrifying silence and uncrossing his legs as he leaned towards her, 'why can't we behave like civilised people towards each other, and have a civilised discussion without all this infernal bickering?'

'Because we belong on opposite sides of the fence,' she replied tritely, evading those eyes that seemed to be boring into hers as if to reach the hidden recesses of her soul.

'That fence is of your own making.'

'No, Jordan.' She shook her head and gripped her hands together so tightly in her lap that they ached. 'Nature made that fence, and I've learnt to accept it.'

'Have you?' he demanded harshly, and when her eyes met his she knew the terrible fear that she might break down and fling herself into his arms to cry out her despair like a child against his solid chest.

'Oh, go away!' she begged in desperation. 'Leave me alone!'

'I'll go away, Margot, but I'll never leave you entirely alone.' His dark, piercing eyes raked over her, taking in her frail slenderness, the unnatural hollows in her cheeks, and the lifeless appearance of her russet-coloured hair as it tumbled about her face. 'God knows why, but I feel a responsibility towards you,' he added, and she stiffened automatically with indignation and anger.

'You have a responsibility towards your mother and towards Berdine. You need never feel a responsibility towards me. I don't expect it of you, and neither do I need it.'

A humourless smile curved his mouth. 'Berdine and my mother are well able to take care of themselves, but you're not.'

'I've always managed perfectly well without you in the past.'

'That may be so,' he shrugged his wide shoulders beneath the superb cut of his grey jacket, 'but you don't seem to have managed very well on your own lately.'

'Perhaps not,' she admitted reluctantly, 'but circumstances have been a little out of the ordinary.'

'Am I included in those "circumstances" you mention?'

'Yes,' she breathed against her will, caught between anger and tears. 'Oh, I wish you'd go!'

'One day, Margot,' he smiled, rising slowly to his feet and leaning over her chair, 'one day you'll beg me to stay, and then I'll remind you of this.'

He was gone before she could think of a suitable reply, but his remark haunted her for some time afterwards.

During the long, lazy weeks of Margot's convalescence she came to know Daniel and Joanne Grant as she had never known them before. Their love for each other was obvious in every look, and every touch, and Margot discovered, too, that young Serena was not only the product of their love for each other, but the veritable apple of her father's eye. Margot herself felt drawn into the warm circle of their love, but it often left her with the feeling of emptiness that originated from the aching need for a home and a family of her own.

Berdine Powell had returned to Cape Town during this time without the announcement of her engagement being made public, but Margot understood that she would be returning to Willowmead towards the beginning of summer with the intention of staying over for the Christmas season.

*Christmas!* It was barely six weeks away, but Margot did not even want to think of it yet. It would be her first Christmas without her mother, and heaven only knew how she was going to live through the festive season without those little surprises they had always prepared for each other.

Her mind dwelled on many subjects while she lay on the recliner in the quiet garden, and it was inevitable that Jordan should invade her thoughts. No matter how much she tried, she could not wrench him from her mind, for she knew that soon, too soon perhaps, he would be celebrating something of quite a different nature, and that was something she dared not stay to witness.

A shadow fell across her, and she opened her eyes reluctantly to find herself staring up at the object of her thoughts. Her pulse rate quickened alarmingly as her gaze travelled over him, for in beige corded pants and thin matching sweater, he emanated that aura of raw masculinity which never failed to attack her senses.

This was the first time in all the weeks of her convalescence at the Grant home that she found herself entirely alone with Jordan, and it was this thought that frightened her into saying stupidly, 'Daniel and Joanne aren't at home.'

'I know,' he replied, smiling that mocking smile which she knew she would associate with him for the rest of her life. 'That's why I'm here.'

'To keep an eye on me?' she demanded sarcastically.

'Among other things, yes.'

'Other things?' she questioned at once, alert and suspicious as he brushed aside the folds of her skirt to seat himself beside her on the recliner. 'What other things?' she asked, moving her legs unobtrusively to give him more room.

Jordan took a long time replying as his dark glance played over her with mocking intent, taking in the healthy, newly-acquired tan of her smooth skin, the flush on cheeks which had filled out once more, and wide grey eyes fringed with long, dark lashes; lashes that fluttered down moments later to hide the emotions mirrored there.

'I suppose it would surprise you to learn that I enjoy your company, and even though you may be prejudiced and obstinate, I've never yet found you boring,' he announced, and those long lashes flew upwards once more to reveal eyes sparkling with anger when they met his.

'You consider me an antidote to boredom?'

'There, you see,' he laughed briefly. 'I knew you'd rise to the occasion.'

Wariness replaced the anger in her glance, and she sighed, 'Did you come here purposely to upset me?'

'Heaven forbid I should do that!'

Margot stared down at the magazine which she had not bothered to read, and she was amazed at the steadiness of her hands when her insides were shaking with that intense awareness his presence always evoked.

'Why *did* you come, then?'

'Because I couldn't stay away.'

'Don't be silly,' she laughed nervously, shifting her position carefully once again to avoid the touch of his hard thigh against her hip.

'I'm serious,' Jordan insisted, and when she scraped together enough courage to raise her eyes to his, she found that he was exactly that.

He leaned towards her, his one hand pressing into the recliner, imprisoning her, while with the other he explored the curve of her cheek, her throat, and her reddish-brown hair which fell softly about her face, but when those sensitive fingers probed the vulnerable area behind her ear, she felt that she could bear it no more.

'Jordan . . .' she begged a little breathlessly, the magazine falling from her nerveless fingers to lie unheeded on the grass, 'don't do this to me.'

He smiled as his thumbs probed the delicate bones above the collar of her blouse where her pulse throbbed madly at the base of her throat. 'I haven't done anything to you yet.'

'What do you want of me?' she asked, the huskiness in her voice accentuated by the unwanted sensations spiralling through her.

'I want nothing you're not prepared to give,' he assured her, while the clean male smell of him, and the sensuality of those clever fingers blended to become a potent combination that made her quiver with the emotions he had aroused. 'Don't tremble so, Margot,' he warned softly. 'It's a temptation to hold you in my arms.'

'Then why don't you go away and leave me in peace?' she groaned helplessly.

'I can't do that,' Jordan ground out the words, his

eyes darkening with a desire that found a delirious response in her. 'Dammit, Margot, you know I can't!'

'Jordan . . .' she sighed against his mouth, 'I sometimes think you possess all the qualities of the devil himself.'

He laughed softly, tempting her with feather-light kisses until her lips finally parted of their own volition beneath his. His bulk blotted out the sun, and the world spun crazily about her while they kissed and clung as if they had hungered a long time for just this moment. Through the silky thinness of her blouse his hands caressed her breasts, and they swelled eagerly to his touch.

'I want you, Margot,' he murmured hoarsely when his mouth left hers at last to begin a sensual exploration against the smoothness of her sensitive throat. 'Let me take you away somewhere quiet where we could be entirely alone.'

Margot plunged from her high peak of ecstasy as if someone had pushed her forcibly over the edge and, mentally winded, it was some time before she was able to struggle free of his arms.

'No! No, I can't!' she cried, 'and you have no right to expect it of me!'

Her hands were against his chest where she could feel the hard, wild beat of his heart beneath her palms as she held him off, and he released her almost at once, the glazed look in his eyes replaced now by a dark fury.

'I swear, Margot, I've never met anyone like you before!'

Hiding her emotional vulnerability behind a shield of anger, she asked sharply, 'You mean you've never before met a woman capable of resisting you?'

'Yes!' he almost shouted at her in the fury of his

obvious frustration and anger. 'Yes, you're right! I've never met a woman I haven't been able to persuade into bed with me at some time or another!'

'I'm sure it didn't take much to persuade Berdine.'

'That's none of your business!'

His lashing remark had slammed the door securely in her face, and she knew a deep sense of remorse when she surfaced through the pain of it.

'I'm sorry,' she whispered, biting down hard on her trembling lip. 'I had no right to say that.'

'Oh, God!'

She stared at him in dismay when he buried his head in his hands in a peculiar attitude of defeat which was oddly touching, and she reached out a tentative hand to touch his arm. 'Jordan?'

He brushed off her hand as if her touch disgusted him, and rose to his feet. 'I'd better go before I say something I know I shall regret for the rest of my life.'

'Jordan, I—I don't understand you,' she sighed.

'That's not surprising,' he lashed out at her. 'You're so wrapped up in your cocoon of prejudice that you totally lack that spark of human understanding most people would expect from a woman of your intelligence.'

Margot flinched as if he had struck her physically, and she felt raw and bruised inwardly as she watched him striding away from her across the lawn. The indecision she had been plagued with recently was suddenly no longer there, and she knew what she had to do, but she would have to act swiftly before she was tempted to change her mind.

## CHAPTER EIGHT

EVA MERRICK arrived at Joanne's home on an unexpected visit one afternoon, and Margot could not
help thinking it rather odd, for Eva Merrick and Joanne
seemed to have very little to say to each other. Awkward little silences seemed to be the order of the day,
but the reason for her sobering presence was finally
made clear to Margot when Joanne went inside to prepare a tray for tea. Left alone on the terrace with the
autocratic old lady, Margot felt ill at ease and tempted
to excuse herself on some pretext or other, but those
cold eyes, surveying her with undisguised distaste, held
her pinned to her chair for seemingly endless seconds
while she prayed desperately for Joanne to hurry up
with the tea.

'I realise that this is none of my business, of course,'
Eva Merrick began, 'but you seem perfectly well to me,
and I wondered ...' she paused dramatically before
coming to the point '... don't you think you have
rather outstayed your welcome in Dr Grant's home?'

Momentarily staggered by the swiftness of her attack,
Margot could only stare at her blankly for a few
seconds, then she gathered her wits about her and said
with equal chilliness, 'Don't you think, Mrs Merrick,
that it's for Joanne to say whether she wants me to stay
or not?'

'My dear,' the older woman smiled that humourless
smile, 'Joanne is merely allowing you to stay because
she feels obliged to do so, and you know yourself that,

socially, you don't really belong here.'

'If Margot doesn't belong here, Mrs Merrick, then neither do I,' Joanne interceded unexpectedly in an icy voice that Margot had never heard her use before as she stepped out on to the terrace and placed the tray of tea on the low, cane table, then she straightened and faced Eva Merrick squarely with a gleam of defiance in her green eyes. 'My father was nothing but a departmental clerk and, but for Daniel's position in this community, it's quite likely that I wouldn't have been accepted into your social circle.'

'Well, really!' Eva Merrick almost choked on the words.

'Furthermore, Mrs Merrick,' Joanne continued, undaunted, 'Margot is my guest for as long as she cares to stay, and I shall expect you to treat her with the respect she deserves.'

'That's just it!' Eva Merrick exclaimed, her thin cheeks red with anger. 'Her father was a steam engine driver or some such thing, while her mother was nothing but a common dressmaker. What respect, I ask you, does the offspring of such a couple deserve?'

'My father made an honest living while he was alive, and so did my mother,' Margot exploded, shaking with fury. 'They earned their fair share of respect without having to pay a cent for it, and I won't have you speak of them as if they were some kind of obnoxious weed!'

'That's a typical reaction from someone who was born into the kind of hovel you're accustomed to,' Mrs Merrick snapped viciously.

'That will do!' Joanne insisted coldly before Margot could get another word in edgeways. 'I will not have Margot insulted here in my home, and you will treat her with as much politeness as you would anyone else from this side of town.'

'I will not be dictated to, and if that's what you expect of me, then I shan't be staying to tea,' Eva Merrick announced haughtily, rising to her feet with a look of injured dignity on her face. 'Good day to you!'

'You left something, Mrs Merrick,' Margot called after her, picking up the forgotten gloves on the small table beside the chair where Jordan's mother had sat.

The woman turned, her eyes like steel blades of fury piercing Margot's slender form as she snatched the gloves from Margot's hands and marched out towards her car in the driveway.

It was not until they heard her Mercedes speed down the long drive that Margot and Joanne glanced at each other, to become almost convulsed with laughter when they both saw the comical side to the unpleasant incident which had just occurred.

'I shouldn't have lost my temper with her,' Margot sighed with a hint of regret in her voice once they had sobered up. 'Everyone is entitled to their own opinions, and she was right about the fact that I'm no longer so desperately ill. You can't deny, Joanne, that it *is* time I went back to my own home where I belong.'

Joanne's anxious fingers gripped Margot's arm. 'Don't pay any attention to the things she said. She's a supercilious, class-conscious old lady and, thank goodness, one of the few still left here in Willowmead.'

'What really bothers her is that, staying here with you, I'm too close to Jordan for her own comfort,' Margot was forced into admitting.

'Has she ever mentioned anything like that to you?'

'Something like that—once—the day before Berdine put in an appearance,' Margot smiled now with the memory of her meeting with Eva Merrick that Saturday morning in the Protea Tea Room.

'And you told her, of course, that she had nothing to fear from you,' Joanne concluded shrewdly.

'She *has* no reason to fear me in that respect.'

'Is that why you always keep Jordan at——'

'Stop it, Joanne!' Margot interrupted laughingly, but with a hint of severity in her voice. 'The tea's getting cold, and I happen to be thirsty.'

'Sorry, Margot,' Joanne smiled, seating herself in front of the tray and proceeding to pour their tea. 'I won't pry any further, but forgive me if I draw my own conclusions.'

Despite Joanne's protests, Margot returned to her own home two days later, and a week later she managed to persuade Dr Turner that she was well enough to return to work. On her very first day at the clinic, however, Margot put her long-thought-out plans into action and went to see Matron Selby who was surprised by Margot's request, but helpful, and the following Sunday Margot called on Joanne to inform her of her decision.

'I'm leaving Willowmead at the end of this month,' she announced when the right moment presented itself.

'You're what?' Joanne asked, almost choking on her tea. 'Margot, you're not serious!'

'I am,' Margot insisted adamantly. 'Very serious.'

'But why?' Joanne demanded incredulously.

'There's a possibility that I could get myself a theatre job at a private hospital in George, and they have agreed at the clinic to release me as soon as I like. I could, in fact, work two weeks' notice, but I shall need a month to settle things here.'

'But, Margot . . .' Joanne seemed temporarily at a loss for words, then she asked cautiously, 'Is it because of Jordan and Berdine?'

'It would be better all round if I left,' Margot evaded the question.

'Running away won't help, you know,' Joanne remonstrated quietly, placing a gentle hand on Margot's arm. 'I tried it once, and I know.'

'Staying isn't going to help me either,' Margot argued desperately. 'I can't stay and . . .'

'And watch him marry Berdine?' Joanne finished for her with extraordinary understanding, and when Margot nodded dumbly, she added fiercely, 'Then why don't you fight for him instead of always turning away from his innuendoes at a closer relationship?'

'It wouldn't be of any use,' Margot told her bitterly. 'We're worlds apart in every respect.'

'Nonsense!'

'His mother——'

'She's of no importance,' Joanne brushed aside Margot's arguments impatiently.

'Joanne . . .' Margot paused, then she sighed helplessly and confessed, 'He doesn't *love* me! Oh, he wants me, yes, for a flirtation or an affair, but *love*?' She shook her head and bit down hard on her lip. 'It's no use, don't you see?'

'You could be mistaken, you know.'

'I doubt it.'

'If I can't persuade you to stay, then you could at least promise me that you won't be in too much of a hurry to leave,' Joanne pleaded.

'I can't promise you anything,' Margot sighed tiredly. 'All I'm sure of at the moment is that I want to be gone before Christmas.'

Jordan confronted Margot alone in her office the following morning before they were to go into the theatre, and she guessed at once what he had on his mind.

'I understand you're leaving us at the end of the month,' he said in a clipped voice, confirming her suspicions.

'That's right.'

'What made you decide to take such a drastic step in your efforts to avoid me?' he demanded sharply, his eyes boring into hers in that disturbing way that always seemed to affect the regular pace of her heart. 'Haven't I been staying out of your way lately, and haven't I done my best to avoid friction between us?'

'Yes, you have,' she admitted reluctantly, then, when she glimpsed that hint of mockery in his eyes, she added untruthfully, 'My resignation has nothing to do with you.'

'Then prove it,' he snapped. 'Withdraw your resignation and stay.'

'I—I can't!'

'Then you admit that I'm correct in my assumption?'

'No!'

'You're not only running away from me, Margot, you're running away from life.'

'Jordan ... please ... you know I can't stay,' she begged, only barely succeeding in controlling the tremor in her choked voice.

'I know nothing of the kind, and I shall make it my business to persuade you otherwise,' he told her harshly, leaning towards her across the desk in a threatening manner that made her heart jerk in her breast. 'Don't say I didn't warn you, Margot.'

Jordan's manner changed towards her after that in a subtle, almost indefinable way, and she encountered the full force of his new approach when she was in Joanne's kitchen one Saturday, helping to prepare the salads for the *braai* they had arranged to celebrate Bruce's birthday.

It was Bruce, however, who first came upon her in the kitchen that afternoon, and he placed his arms about her waist in a playful, brotherly fashion she could not take exception to.

'How's my favourite girl?' he asked, smiling down at her.

'I've missed your funny face,' she told him laughingly, aiming a light blow at his chin with her fist.

'You've made my day, and I just love you, Margot,' he announced, lifting her off her feet and swinging her round despite her amused protestations.

'I dare say that you do love her,' a censorious voice remarked from the doorway, and Bruce set her down at once to turn and stare at Jordan with that hint of merriment still twinkling in his grey eyes. 'You're required to stir the fires outside, not here in the kitchen,' Jordan added.

'Oh, damn, I was asked to bring out the salt, but I was sidetracked by this lovely lady,' Bruce laughed, gesturing with mock fear as he snatched up the salt container, but at the door he turned and raised his hand in salute. 'See you later, sweetheart.'

'Do I congratulate you, or do I offer you my sympathies?' Jordan wanted to know as he approached the table where Margot was covering up her embarrassment by adding the finishing touches to the salad.

'Neither,' she said, surfacing from her forced concentration to thrust two bowls of salad into his hands. 'Take these outside if you want to make yourself useful.'

'On one condition,' he stated calmly, his eyes laughing down into hers.

'And that is?' she demanded suspiciously.

'That I get a kiss for my trouble.'

Laughter, incredulity and anger mingled on her expressive face as she stood there staring up at him, then she reacted in the only possible way by removing the bowls from his hands, and saying lightly, 'I think I'll take them out myself.'

It was a mistake; she realised that a fraction of a second too late. With her hands fully occupied, she was defenceless against the strong muscled arms encircling her waist, and she was drawn hard up against his body while his lips captured hers in a brief yet shattering kiss.

'I'll carry these out for you now,' he announced the moment he released her and, removing the bowls from her trembling hands, he strode towards the door.

'You beast!' she cried out accusingly at his broad back, but he merely glanced at her over his shoulder and laughed mockingly.

'One good turn deserves another, they say.'

It was quite some time before Margot recovered her composure sufficiently in order to go out and face the rest of Joanne's guests, and it was with a sense of shock that she discovered Berdine among them. No one had warned her of Berdine's return to Willowmead, and seeing her draped on Jordan's arm, in a manner that suggested a certain intimacy, left a bitter taste of jealousy in Margot's mouth. Eva Merrick was there as well, her cold smile triumphant as she intercepted Margot's glance, and her expression stating clearly, 'You don't stand a chance.'

There was plenty of laughter around the fires that night. The men drank their beer while they turned the meat on the fires, and the women clustered together in small groups to discuss the latest bit of gossip to hit the village. It was the usual thing at functions such as this, but it was harmless and often enjoyable.

When darkness fell Daniel proposed that they raised their glasses to Bruce to wish him happiness and prosperity for the year ahead, then they helped themselves to the smoky, spiced meat, and carefully prepared salads which had been laid out in the well-lit area of the garden where Daniel and Joanne had chosen to have the *braai*. Bruce was at Margot's side, the gold cigarette case she had given him in his shirt pocket, and his flippant conversation amused her, and kept her attention from wandering too often towards the small group seated beyond the fire where the dying embers glowed a bright red.

It was not until much later that evening that Margot found herself alone for a few minutes, but she was not alone for long when a deep, vibrant voice directly behind her asked mockingly, 'Am I forgiven?'

'Forgiven, Jordan?' she asked lightly, feigning innocence as she turned to face him when he sat down on his heels beside her with an elbow resting on the arm of her chair. 'What for?' she demanded.

'Forgotten so soon?' he questioned mockingly, his smile deepening when he saw the tell-tale colour surge up into her cheeks.

'I prefer not to think about it,' she stated with a calmness she was far from experiencing.

'Was it so distasteful?'

'No, but——' She broke off sharply, but too late. She had stepped neatly into the trap he had set for her, and helpless laughter bubbled from her lips before she could prevent it. 'You devil!' she accused. 'You tricked me into saying that!'

'The truth has a habit of coming out when one least

expects it,' he told her with a sobriety which contradicted the mockery in his dark, glittering eyes.

'Jordan, you're impossible!' she sighed, leaning a little away from him. 'I don't think I know you in this devilish mood you're in.'

'Does it please you?'

'Your mood, you mean?' she asked with mock innocence.

'Naturally.'

Did it please her? she wondered distractedly, taking in his tanned, chiselled features. It certainly excited her in the most peculiar way, but it was an excitement which she knew only too well could lead nowhere for her and, deciding to play safe, she said carefully, 'I—don't quite know how I feel about it, but I'll tell you some other time.'

'When?' he demanded with an odd inflection in his voice as he leaned a bit closer to her. 'Tonight?'

'Next year, perhaps,' she laughed, adopting a teasing manner to match his.

'Too long,' he insisted. 'It will have to be tonight.'

She shook her head adamantly. 'Not tonight.'

'Tomorrow?' he persisted, his hand brushing against her thigh and sending a shiver of sensations along her receptive nerves.

'Stop it, Jordan,' she pleaded softly. 'You're drawing attention to us.'

'Who cares?' he said, his hand tightening on her knee.

'I care, and so does Berdine.'

'Ah, yes, the lovely Berdine,' he sighed, glancing towards the woman who was obviously watching them closely despite the number of men clustered about her. 'I think she's drawing quite enough attention to herself, don't you?'

'Women like Berdine always do draw attention to themselves.'

'Careful,' he warned humorously, 'your claws are showing!'

'I meant it well, believe me,' she answered him with quiet sincerity. 'She's beautiful and intelligent, and she'll make you an admirable wife.'

Jordan studied her for a moment in thoughtful silence before he asked, 'Do you really think so?'

'Yes, I do,' she replied, looking everywhere but into those keen, rapier-sharp eyes observing her so closely.

'Do you think I deserve her?'

'That's not for me to say.'

'You sidestepped that one very nicely, I must say,' he laughed shortly, but without humour, and Margot smiled faintly.

'I'm getting rather good at it, don't you think?'

'Would you like to see me married to her?'

The question was swift and unexpected, and it sliced deep into her soul, but she replied with an honesty which came from the depths of her heart. 'I would like to see you happy, Jordan.'

'I'm very glad you said that,' he remarked after a momentary pause, then he raised her hand and brushed his lips against her fingers. 'See you later.'

Bewildered, she stared after his tall frame. What exactly had he meant by that last remark? she wondered, but the answer evaded her infuriatingly.

She was not surprised, however, when Berdine approached her later that evening and asked to speak to her alone. Margot excused herself from Bruce, and when they were a little distance away from him, Berdine said in her deceptively lilting voice, 'Shall we walk a little this way? I have something rather important to say to you in private.'

The topic of conversation would naturally be Jordan, and Margot needed no prize for guessing this correctly while she walked silently beside Berdine into the shadows of the trees.

'I think we've gone far enough,' Margot announced eventually. 'What you have to say to me can be said right here.'

'Very well,' Berdine agreed, and Margot could not help noticing that her hair was almost silver in the moonlight, while her skin had an alabaster quality which was enviable. 'I would like to suggest that you be a little more careful in future,' she continued. 'You're making your feelings noticeably clear to myself and everyone else, and soon Jordan, too, may begin to notice.'

A cold, sick feeling gripped Margot's insides. 'I don't know what you're talking about.'

'Of course you do,' Berdine laughed softly, but her laughter struck a further chill into Margot's heart. 'You're in love with him, and I've known it for a long time, but don't allow him to suspect it, my dear. It would embarrass him to know that you'd taken his flirtations seriously, and it would embarrass you as well.' She smiled a sweet, venomous smile. 'Have I made myself clear?'

'Perfectly.'

'Someone had to warn you, Margot, and I considered it best that it should come from me. You see,' Berdine smiled again, 'someone of your social background shouldn't expect more than a flirtatious affair from a man such as Jordan.'

That was a deliberate blow below the belt and, feeling sick to the very core of her being, Margot muttered, 'I think you've said enough.'

Eva Merrick had done well in training the woman Jordan was to marry, Margot thought bitterly, keeping to the shadows as she stumbled across the garden towards the house where she knew she would find Joanne in the kitchen making a tray of coffee for their guests, but she collided, unfortunately, with Bruce on the terrace.

'What's the rush?' he asked laughingly as he steadied her, but his expression sobered when he noticed how pale she had gone. 'Is something wrong?'

'I have a splitting headache,' she lied.

'I hope that doesn't mean you're leaving?'

'I'm afraid it does,' she admitted, forcing a smile to her lips and kissing him lightly on the cheek. 'I'm sorry, Bruce.'

An unnatural calmness settled about Margot when she finally confronted Joanne in the kitchen. 'Would you object terribly if I excused myself and went home?' she asked.

'Margot? Has something happened to upset you?' Joanne asked, her glance filled with concern. 'You're quite pale.'

'I have a terrible headache,' Margot explained again, and this time it was not entirely a lie, for her temples were throbbing as if someone were beating a sledgehammer against them.

'You wouldn't like to go upstairs and lie down, would you?'

'No,' Margot shook her head, but the movement made her wince. 'I'd prefer to go home, if you don't mind.'

'Of course I don't mind, Margot. Perhaps you've been doing too much too soon,' Joanne concluded, her glance sharpening. 'Will you manage on your own, or shall I ask Bruce to take you home?'

'No, no, please,' Margot protested hastily. 'I'll manage on my own, and thank you for everything.'

She was never quite certain afterwards how she managed to drive herself home that evening, but when she stepped inside her house and locked the door behind her, her calmness deserted her, and a cold, illogical anger took possession of her. She had not deserved Berdine's stinging remarks. Or ... had she, perhaps?

'Oh, lord,' she grooaned softly into the darkness. 'Am I making it so painfully obvious to everyone that I love Jordan?'

It was a disquieting thought, and it was with this that she went to bed to lie awake most of the night, reliving each incident at Joanne's home, and wondering if, perhaps, Berdine had been right after all.

When the sun finally spread its rosy glow over the awakening earth on that warm Sunday morning in the valley, Margot stood in front of the kitchen window with a mug of coffee between her hands, and she had decided, once and for all, that her plans to leave Willowmead would definitely come to fruition.

She hoped, too, that the unfortunate happenings of the previous evening were over and done with, but when she encountered Eva Merrick's regal presence on her doorstep later that morning, she experienced a sinking feeling that it had only just begun.

'Won't you come in, please, Mrs Merrick?' Margot heard herself say in a voice that sounded surprisingly calm.

'I wouldn't have come if I didn't consider it important,' the older woman remarked assertingly once they were seated in the small lounge, making doubly certain that Margot was aware of the fact that wild dogs would not have dragged her to this side of town had it not been for some extremely valid reason.

'I realise that,' Margot replied, relying heavily on her training as a nurse to maintain an outwardly calm appearance, but inwardly she was a churning mass of nerves.

'I came specifically to discuss your behaviour last night.'

Margot stiffened. '*My* behaviour?'

'Don't put on an act with me!' Eva Merrick stormed at her in that cold, almost malicious voice. 'I considered it atrocious the way you flirted with Jordan!'

'Flirted?' Margot echoed, almost choking on the word. 'I assure you, Mrs Merrick, that I never flirted with——'

'Are you calling me a liar?' the other woman interrupted with a dignified shriek. 'Did you think that no one noticed the way you enticed and encouraged him away from Berdine?'

'But I never encouraged him in——'

'Your behaviour was an insult to Berdine, and a deliberate attempt to cause trouble between her and Jordan. She's an extremely intelligent and sensitive person, but, despite everything, she's willing to forgive your behaviour since she does not want to see you hurt.' Eva Merrick snorted disdainfully. 'Her concern for your feelings is quite ridiculous, of course.'

Margot flinched inwardly. Was she not supposed to have any feelings at all? she wondered cynically as she faced this woman who had declared herself her enemy.

'I doubt very much whether Berdine has concern for anyone's feelings except her own, but if my behaviour has in some way insulted her, then I shall apologise to her personally. I can only assure you, Mrs Merrick, that I was not flirting with Jordan last night, and I did not go out of my way to encourage him. It was he who approached me, and——'

'Are you suggesting that it was Jordan who flirted with you?' Those grey eyes were bitingly hard as they raked Margot scornfully. 'He has never been very selective in his choice of women, but he would never stoop so low—not with trash like you!'

Margot blinked at the insult, and her hands tightened in her lap in an effort to control herself. 'Mrs Merrick ... I think, perhaps, this conversation has gone far enough.'

Eva Merrick was not in the mood to be stunted and, seated on the edge of the chair with her back ramrod-stiff, she launched another attack. 'You knew the situation very well, I had gone to the trouble of making it clear to you myself, and Berdine is——'

'Berdine is on her way back to Cape Town,' a deep voice announced quietly from the door, 'and if I were you, Mother, I would take great care in what you say to Margot. You're speaking to the woman I intend making my wife.'

# CHAPTER NINE

THE electrifying silence in the lounge was so acute that the crowing of the neighbours' fowls sounded as if it had been amplified ten times its normal volume, but for Margot, who had risen shakily to her feet to confront Jordan, it felt as if she had been suspended over a crater's edge on a thin rope which threatened to snap at any moment. Someone had stepped beyond the point of sanity, and she suspected that it was she herself when the mad desire to laugh hysterically rose sharply within her.

Eva Merrick was the first, however, to recover her composure and, rising to her feet with a dignity Margot could not help but admire, she faced her son across the room.

'Have you gone out of your mind?' she demanded stonily.

'No, Mother,' he assured her in a tight-lipped fashion. 'I happened to hear most of what you said to Margot, and I can only repeat that it would be wise of you to heed my warning.'

'You can't be serious, Jordan!' she exclaimed, a little frantic now as she glanced at Margot and added scornfully, 'You can't marry this—this girl!'

'Why don't you go home, Mother, and leave us alone to sort out our lives without interference from you.'

Eva Merrick's colour alternated between white and purple, and finally settled for a sickly white. 'You'll regret this, Jordan,' she warned shrilly. 'You mark my words, you'll regret it!'

'No, Mother,' he contradicted sharply as he stepped farther into the lounge. '*You* will regret it if you don't go home and think things over carefully.'

'Well!' she exclaimed indignantly as she picked up her handbag and marched towards the door. 'I never thought I'd live to see the day when my own son would speak to me in this manner, and you may as well know that I blame this common hussy for it!'

'*That's enough!*'

The lash in Jordan's voice made Margot want to shrivel up and die, but Eva Merrick merely snorted and marched out of the house. She slammed the door behind her and drove away in a cloud of dust with fowls scattering in all directions and squawking loudly at having their leisurely stroll across the street disturbed in this rude manner.

At any other time this incident might have been amusing, Margot realised as she glanced out of the window and watched the dust and feathers settle, but at that moment she felt sick with incredible anger. She had endured enough at the hands of the Merrick family to last her a lifetime.

'You had no right telling your mother that you intended marrying me, because you know it's not true!' she stormed at Jordan, but he stood there rock-like, his calmness merely increasing her fury.

'You mean I should have asked you first?'

'I mean it's totally out of the question,' she spat out the words. 'Marriage was the farthest thing from your mind until you overheard your mother's insulting remarks, and you can't deny it!'

'No, I don't deny it!' he confessed harshly as he lessened the distance between them in one lithe stride, 'but you might as well know that I intend making you my wife even if it takes me the rest of my life.'

'It might very well take you an eternity!' she hissed at him emphatically, backing away in order to keep a safe distance between them. 'I wouldn't marry you even if you were the last eligible man left on this earth!'

'Margot——'

'Don't touch me!' she warned heatedly as he reached for her. 'I've taken about as much as I can stand from you, your mother, and your precious Berdine, and I *hate* you. Do you understand?' Her voice was hoarse with the intensity of the fury that raged through her. 'I hate you and *everything* you stand for, and *nothing* you could do or say would ever persuade me to marry you!'

'Hate is a strong word,' he mocked her, his jaw hard and his muscled body alert as if he were geared for action at a moment's notice.

'Hate may be a strong word, but that's the way I feel about this entire situation,' she cried, choking back her tears, and fighting for the control which was fast slipping away from her. 'I'm sick to death of it all, and I hope I never have to see you again unless I absolutely have to. Between you and your mother you've killed every scrap of liking and respect I still had for you. I've been humiliated and insulted enough, and I won't tolerate it a moment longer, do you hear?'

Jordan's broad shoulders moved slightly beneath the splendid cut of his lightweight jacket. 'You don't mean what you're saying, Margot.'

'I mean every word,' she insisted, blind to the peculiar whiteness that had settled about his mouth. 'I couldn't care less if our paths never cross again, and I hope to God that, after the end of this month, they never do.'

'Do you know what you're doing?'

'Yes!' she cried, her voice rising with hysteria. 'I know exactly what I'm doing. I'm telling you to go, and I couldn't put it more plainly than that. I want you out of my life, and I want you to stay out of it!'

She turned away, rejecting what she had once wanted so desperately, but she could not live with the knowledge that his offer of marriage had been made merely to thwart and aggravate his mother, and her back was rigid with the effort to control the desolation that swept through her when she finally heard his Mercedes being driven at speed down the dusty street.

Not once had Jordan indicated that he felt anything other than desire for her, and desire was not enough. She had wanted his love, but what would she have done if he had said he loved her? Would she not still have been convinced that a marriage between them was out of the question? They came from opposite sides of the village, and they belonged in different spheres of society; a society with prejudices on both sides, perhaps, but prejudices which were kept alive by Eva Merrick and the few who still believed, as she did, that the two sides should never mix socially.

'Oh, now what am I going to do?' she asked herself, but the question was irrelevant. She would be leaving Willowmead within two weeks, and then, with any luck, she would never have to see Jordan again.

Margot drove out to see Joanne that afternoon, and was relieved to discover that Daniel and Bruce had taken a boat out on to the river. She needed someone to talk to; to confide in, but when they sat out on the lawn with Serena playing happily at their feet with her toys, Margot found she could not speak of the things which had hurt her so deeply. The words became locked in her throat, forcing her to silence, and she was left with the task of carrying her burden alone.

Joanne poured their tea, and it was inevitable that the discussion would turn to the *braai* the previous evening.

'It's such a pity you had to leave early last night,' Joanne remarked with a teasing light in her eyes. 'Bruce was absolutely devasted by your absence, and I can think of at least one other person who felt the same.'

This was Margot's opportunity to confide in Joanne, but once again the words became strangled in her throat, and her despairing glance went involuntarily towards the Merrick house which was partially hidden behind the cypress and chestnut trees. Alarm, more than curiosity, made her rise up out of her chair moments later to stare in that direction more intently.

'Is that smoke coming from one of the upstairs windows of the Merrick house?' she anxiously sought confirmation from Joanne.

'Dear God, yes!' Joanne exclaimed, her cup clattering into the tray as she leapt to her feet. 'It's coming from Mrs Merrick's bedroom.'

'Do you think Jordan is aware of it?'

'Jordan isn't home, I believe, and neither are the servants,' Joanne explained hurriedly, 'and if I'm not mistaken, this is the time of day when Mrs Merrick usually takes a nap.'

Margot had sworn, once, never to set foot on Merrick soil again, but this was an emergency, and her reaction was instinctive.

'Call the fire department,' she rapped out an order to Joanne. 'I'm going to make sure that Mrs Merrick's not in any danger.'

'Don't do anything foolish,' Joanne warned anxiously, lifting a wriggling Serena into her arms and dashing inside to the telephone, but Margot barely heard her, for she was already sprinting across the lawn towards the small opening in the hedge dividing their homes.

The volume of smoke pouring from the window seemed to increase with every passing second as Margot dashed across the once familiar garden towards the house. Her prayers were answered when she found the front door unlocked, and she burst into the house to take the stairs two at a time. On the top landing she paused for a moment to regain her sense of direction, but she did not waste another second when she glimpsed smoke curling from beneath a door to her left.

When she entered the heated, smoke-filled room, the draught of air increased the speed with which the smouldering fire was spreading across the thick pile of the carpet, and it was rapidly approaching the inert figure lying on the floor beside the bed. Smoke stung her eyes and nose as she knelt beside Eva Merrick's unconscious form, her hands seeking hastily for further injuries, and, satisfied that she had merely been overcome by the fumes, Margot dragged her as quickly as she could from the room into the passage which was already filling up with the foul-smelling fumes. The woman was a dead weight, but Margot managed to prop her up against the wall before she turned back to close the bedroom door, hoping to contain the fire in this manner until help arrived.

Eva Merrick coughed and spluttered, but she did not quite regain consciousness, and Margot was deliberating how she was going to manage on her own when Joanne appeared on the landing. Between the two of them they somehow managed to carry the unconscious woman down the stairs and out on to the lawn where the air was fresh, but Margot could not leave it at that.

'Take care of her, Joanne,' she said anxiously. 'I'm going back to do something about that fire.'

'Margot, you can't——' Joanne started to protest, but Margot did not stay to be persuaded out of what she knew she had to do.

Armed with a towel which she had soaked in one of the upstairs bathrooms, Margot took a deep breath and burst into Eva Merrick's bedroom. Acrid smoke filled her eyes and nose as she frantically tried to put out the fire which had progressed to the stage where flames were licking at the furniture. Her lungs felt as though they wanted to burst, but there was no time to draw breath, nor to consider the consequences. She had to continue with her efforts to keep the fire under control until help arrived, she decided a little hysterically, but the next moment she was horrified to see the curtains at the window catch alight. The sound of approaching sirens was in her ears as she made use of every ounce of strength she possessed to tear down the curtains and beat out the flames. The fumes choked her, and she was coughing raspingly until it felt as though the fire had penetrated into her lungs and beyond. Stinging tears streamed from her smoke-filled eyes, and she went down on her knees as the room began to whirl about her.

'I must get out of here,' she thought weakly, a coughing spasm tearing at her insides as she crawled on hands and knees in a desperate effort to reach the door, then everything suddenly went black and she knew no more.

She regained consciousness eventually to find an anxious Joanne bending over her.

'The fire!' Margot cried hoarsely, clutching at her stinging throat.

'Take it easy,' Joanne ordered calmly, her hands gentle but firm as she held Margot down. 'Everything's under control.'

'Mrs Merrick?'

'She's lying comfortably in her hospital bed,' Joanne smiled down at her reassuringly, 'and that's exactly where you are at this moment.'

Margot's bloodshot, bewildered eyes registered for the first time the high, white walls surrounding her. 'What am I doing here?'

'You were overcome by the fumes,' Joanne explained, making her pillows more comfortable and straightening the sheets, then those serious green eyes met Margot's. 'You were really very courageous.'

'It was nothing.' Margot brushed aside the compliment to ask with some urgency, 'Was there much damage?'

'Very little, thanks to you. They suspect that Mrs Merrick's automatic tea-maker caused the fire when it developed an electrical fault, and there was very little for the fire department to do except to get you out of there, and to make sure that the fire wouldn't flare up again,' Joanne told her, and, satisfied, Margot leaned back against the pillows and closed her eyes. 'I'm going to leave you now so you can get some rest,' she heard Joanne say, and then she knew nothing more until she awoke to find Dr Turner bending over her.

She left him to examine her in silence, but when he was finished, she asked: 'When may I go home?'

'You're not leaving here until I'm certain that your lungs are absolutely clear.'

'But I can't——'

'Don't argue, Margot,' he interrupted sternly. 'You suffered a bad bout of pneumonia not so long ago, and we can't afford to take chances with your lungs after you saw fit to pump them so full of fumes with your heroic action.'

'Oh, damn!' she muttered, scowling up at the ceiling.

'Shall I prescribe something for you to help you sleep?'

'I don't think so,' Margot shook her head, coming to terms with the situation. 'Thank you, Dr Turner.'

'I'll call in again tomorrow,' he said, patting her arm lightly as if he understood, and then he was gone.

Before Margot could go to sleep that evening she received yet another visitor. A tired, rather haggard-looking Jordan strolled into her ward unannounced, and she hardened her heart at the sight of him to ask abruptly, 'What do you want?'

'I know I'm not very welcome, but I came to say thank you,' he explained, thrusting his hands into his pockets, and staring down at her with a brooding expression on his face. 'Considering how my mother has treated you, I wouldn't have blamed you if you'd left her in that fire to die.'

Margot suppressed the tremor of shock that rippled through her and said indignantly, 'I don't know what kind of person you take me for, but I could never live with someone's death on my conscience—not even your mother's.'

A tiny muscle jerked at the side of his jaw. 'You really do hate us, don't you.'

It was a statement, not a question, and her hands tightened on the sheets until her knuckles showed white through the skin. 'I'd like to go to sleep, if you don't mind.'

She could not have made it more clear that she wished him to leave, and his tight-lipped expression told her that he was aware of this as he turned from her and walked out of her ward.

Jordan's visit had upset her more than she was prepared to admit, and it was a long time before she was able to shed the effect he had had on her in order to drift into a disturbed, fitful sleep.

Matron Selby called to see Margot the following evening, and although she was surprised, she was extraordinarily accommodating when Margot requested a transfer from the theatre to night duty on the wards for the duration of her stay at the clinic. Sister Lewis was coping perfectly in the theatre and, as it was, Margot considered herself superfluous. These were naturally the reasons Margot offered Matron Selby, but she kept to herself the fact that a change of this nature would quite likely seldom necessitate a meeting between Jordan and herself.

'It's been quite a considerable time since you did night duty on the wards, Sister Huntley,' Matron warned. 'Do you think you'll be able to cope?'

'I would welcome the change,' Margot assured her, and Matron nodded in her usual abrupt fashion.

'We could do with a little extra help at night,' she admitted, remaining only long enough to admire the flowers Joanne and Bruce had brought Margot that afternoon before she excused herself and went home.

Margot was allowed out of hospital on the Tuesday morning, but when she passed Eva Merrick's ward and saw her lying propped up against the pillows, her compassionate heart would not let her pass without enquiring after the health of the woman she had dragged from that smoke-filled room.

'I gather you saved my life,' Mrs Merrick remarked haughtily before Margot had the opportunity to speak.

'I suppose I ought to be grateful to you for that at least.'

Margot stiffened at the foot of the autocratic old lady's bed. 'I merely did what anyone else would have done under similar circumstances, Mrs Merrick.'

Those grey eyes surveyed Margot without the slightest sign of softening. 'I hope you don't imagine that this will alter the situation.'

'You're perfectly entitled to your opinions, Mrs Merrick, and it was not my intention to change them.'

'I'm very glad to hear you say that.' There was an awkward little silence, but as Margot was about to leave, Mrs Merrick stopped her with, 'I believe you were sensible enough to turn Jordan down.'

It was with mixed feelings that Margot stared down at the old woman reclining against the pillows in her bedjacket of expensive lace. She wanted to hate her, but she could not. She felt sorry for her instead and, without realising it, her voice took on a gentler note as she said: 'Jordan mentioned marriage merely to annoy you.'

Eva Merrick's thin face hardened. 'That is so, yes.'

Those words pierced Margot's heart ruthlessly. It was one thing to suspect something, but it was quite another to have one's suspicions confirmed and, stepping away from the bed, she said thickly, 'I hope you'll soon be well enough to return home, Mrs Merrick.'

Eva Merrick did not make an effort to detain her, and neither did Margot expect her to. Their conversation was at an end, just as many things would soon come to an end, and after that there would be nothing left for Margot but the bleak emptiness of the future.

The days passed uneventfully for Margot, but not without some painful moments, such as when she caught a brief glimpse of Jordan when she came off duty one morning.

She had been walking towards the parking area with a group of nurses when he had strode past, but he had not looked her way, and moments later he had entered the building without so much as a casual glance in her direction. It had been foolish of her to feel hurt about it, most especially after she had been so adamant about wanting nothing more to do with him, but she could not help herself. She loved him, despite everything, and there was nothing she could do to alter that.

When she came off night duty for the last time, with her departure from Willowmead hanging over her like a sombre cloud, she found an envelope pinned to the notice board in the foyer, and it was addressed to her personally. It was from the Chief Surgeon, and it stated simply, 'See me in my office this morning, stat. D. Grant.'

Frowning, Margot crossed the foyer and walked down the short passage towards Daniel's office. She knocked briefly, and his gravelly voice commanded her to enter at once.

Seated behind his desk Daniel was no longer a friend, but the Chief Surgeon of the Willowmead Clinic, and someone with an obvious problem, she noticed as she stood with her hands locked respectfully behind her back.

'We regret losing your services, Margot,' he said abruptly, and she flashed him a quick, nervous smile.

'I regret leaving, but it's best this way.'

'I'm concerned about Jordan,' he said without further hesitation. 'His work is not up to its usual standard, and he appears to be distracted.'

'I fail to see why you should feel it necessary to mention this to me, Dr Grant,' Margot answered quietly, hiding her shocked concern successfully as she afforded this man the respect due to him despite the fact that he had become 'Daniel' to her during her convalescence.

'I was hoping you could shed some light on the situation.' Those deep blue eyes pinned her ruthlessly to the floor. 'Am I wrong in thinking that you care for him?'

His question drew a gasp of surprise from her that she could not conceal entirely, and her colour deepened. 'My feelings don't come into this, surely?'

'That depends,' he said, his features remaining stern. 'If something has happened between you to affect his work in this manner, then I suggest strongly that you set it right at once before something happens which might necessitate my asking for his resignation.'

'Oh, no!' Her cry was a plea. 'You wouldn't do that! You couldn't!'

'I might have to,' Daniel insisted harshly.

'But he's an absolutely brilliant surgeon!' she argued.

'He *was*,' Daniel corrected abruptly. 'You haven't seen him at work these past weeks.'

'But he——' Margot broke off with an abruptness that matched his and shook her head confusedly. 'I don't understand it.'

'Will you talk to him?'

Margot hesitated. 'Couldn't you?'

'My dear Margot, I already have, but I don't seem to have made much impression, so I'm relying heavily on your assistance in this matter.'

To have refused would have been out of the question; not after everything he and his wife had done for her since her mother's death, and, feeling as though she had been driven into a corner, she said the only thing she could, 'I'll see what I can do, but I—I can't promise you anything definite.'

'All I ask is that you try.' He lit a cigarette and then, as if to stress the seriousness of the situation, he added: 'Jordan's a damned good surgeon, and I'd hate to lose him.'

Margot nodded and Daniel rose at once behind his desk, indicating that the conversation was at an end, but the last half of his remark remained with her as if it had been carved into her brain with a scalpel.

*'I'd hate to lose him.'*

Those had been Daniel's words, but—oh, now, how painfully they echoed through her, wrenching and tearing at her soul as if they were a cry from her own heart.

Jordan had said that he wanted to marry her and, with every part of her being, she had wanted to accept, but she *could* not; not after everything that had happened, and not when she knew that he had done so mainly to anger his mother. There were numerous other reasons why she had refused him, but she did not want to think of them at that moment, for they merely stirred up the bitterness inside her. And now, after everything which had occurred between them; after all the hateful things she had flung at him, it was *she* who had been asked to speak to him in order to bring him to his senses.

Was it her fault that Jordan's work was not up to its usual standard lately? she wondered when she arrived home and made herself a light breakfast that Saturday morning before going to bed and trying to get some sleep. Was it her fault, or had Berdine Powell's departure more to do with it than any of them had realised? What would she say to him? she wondered eventually when she tossed about in her bed. And, worst of all, she wondered frantically how he would receive her.

Margot's jumbled, agitated thoughts did not induce sleep, and she went through to the kitchen eventually to make herself a mug of cocoa. She went to sleep after that, but it was a fitful sleep from which the telephone's shrill ringing awakened her shortly after one o'clock that day.

'I thought you'd like to know,' Joanne's voice said moments after Margot had stumbled sleepily into the passage to lift the receiver, 'Jordan has been involved in an accident.'

Totally awake now, Margot felt as if the blood had drained from her heart to leave her deathly pale as she heard herself repeat faintly, 'An accident?'

'He rolled his car just outside of town, and they've taken him to the hospital,' Joanne explained briefly.

'Oh, God!' Margot thought, closing her eyes and leaning against the wall for support when her legs threatened to cave in beneath her. Visions of Jordan, his magnificent body battered and broken, flashed tormentingly through her mind, and she knew that if anything happened to him after all the dreadful things she had said to him, she would never be able to forgive herself, and neither would she want to continue living.

'Margot?' Joanne's voice penetrated her frightening thoughts. 'Are you still there?'

'Yes—yes, I'm here,' Margot whispered hoarsely. 'How badly was he injured, do you know?'

'I have no idea, I'm afraid,' Joanne replied with a calmness Margot envied. 'Daniel has gone down to the hospital to see him, and he said he'd let me know as soon as there was anything to report, but I haven't heard from him yet.'

'I think I'll go there myself,' Margot announced, making a snap decision, and she replaced the receiver on its cradle almost before Joanne had time to say 'cheerio'.

Margot flew down the passage to her bedroom and, opening her wardrobe, she pulled out the first thing she could lay her hands on. Minutes later, dressed in an old pair of slacks and sweater, she was driving with considerable speed towards the hospital on the outskirts of the town.

The Sister on duty in Casualty was helpful but non-committal. She enlightened Margot as to where they had taken Jordan and, almost without thanking her, Margot stormed out of her office and down several empty passages to collide heavily with a tall, lean frame emerging from one of the wards.

'Daniel!' the man's name burst from her quivering lips as his strong hands shot out to steady her, and she raised anxious grey eyes to his to ask unsteadily, 'Where have they taken him?'

Daniel released her and jerked a thumb towards the door behind him. 'He's through there.'

'How—How is he?' she asked, her heart in her mouth.

'Why don't you go in and see for yourself?'

With her eyes on Daniel's stern face, she asked jerkily, 'Is it that bad?'

His eyebrows rose a fraction, but his expression gave nothing away as he replied with his usual abruptness, 'It could have been worse.'

'Oh!' she groaned, losing the remaining shreds of her composure as she turned to stare at the closed door with something close to fear at the thought of what she would find beyond it.

'Take it easy,' Daniel warned in that gravelly, professional voice. 'You wouldn't want Jordan to see you like this, would you?'

'No, of course not,' she shook her head and, squaring her shoulders, she stepped towards the door and opened it with a trembling hand.

# CHAPTER TEN

MARGOT could never explain afterwards exactly how she felt at that moment when she walked into that room to find Jordan in an upright position while he was being assisted into his jacket by an obliging nurse. Her composure, acquired through long years of training, deserted her completely, and she stepped forward to clutch the railings at the foot of the high bed when she felt herself sway with the intensity of her relief.

Except for the narrow strip of adhesive dressing on the side of his forehead he appeared to be unhurt, but her glance was drawn irrevocably to those dark eyes surveying her intently, and with a measure of surprise, from beneath frowning dark brows.

An eternity seemed to pass before he turned to the nurse hovering beside him. 'Would you leave us alone, please?'

The starched cap bobbed on her head as she nodded assent. 'Certainly, Dr Merrick.'

The door was closed firmly behind her, and again there was that lengthy, terrifying silence during which Margot tried desperately to control the trembling of her limbs.

'Joanne telephoned,' she managed at last in a voice that sounded quite unlike her own. 'She said—she said that——'

'That I'd rolled my car?' he questioned with cynicism curving that strongly sensuous mouth into a hard, twisted line. 'I did, yes, but fortunately I received only a cut on the forehead, and a few minor scratches and bruises which should heal in a few days.'

'They're not keeping you here?' she heard herself asking unnecessarily.

'No, they're not.' His eyes narrowed as they swept her from head to foot, and she had never been more conscious of the cheap linen of her slacks and the inexpensive silk of her sweater. 'For someone who, not two weeks ago, had stated that she wanted nothing more to do with me, you're showing a surprising interest in my welfare,' he reminded her stingingly.

'Don't!' she begged huskily, turning away from him to hide the tears that had sprung unbidden to her eyes, and, in silence, she fought to regain her shattered composure, but she had succeeded only partially when he spoke directly behind her.

'Would you care to give me a lift, considering that I'm without transport at the moment?'

Margot hid her surprise at his request with some difficulty, and nodded, then she led the way out to where she had parked her Mini, and observed him in silence while he eased himself into the passenger seat beside her.

'Where shall I take you?' she asked finally, her hands gripping the steering wheel tightly in an effort to hide the fact that they were shaking.

'To your place,' Jordan said without hesitation, and when she turned to glance at him nervously, he added with quiet self-assurance, 'We have to talk, don't we.'

His eyes challenged her to deny his statement, but she could not and, nodding dumbly, she turned the key in the ignition and the engine sprang to life. She eased her foot off the clutch and accelerated, but her movements were jerky, and the car responded in a similar manner, making Jordan exclaim in something between anger and pain.

'I'm sorry,' Margot said nervously, her hand shaking as she changed gear and, fortunately, the rest of the journey to her home was accomplished without a similar incident occurring, but his large presence in the confined space beside her made her quiver with a certain awareness, and most especially when her hand accidentally brushed against his hard thigh on one occasion when she had to change gear.

'Would you like something to drink?' she asked the moment they were in the small lounge of her home.

'I could do with a stiff tot of whisky.'

'I haven't any whisky in the house, but I do have a bottle of brandy somewhere,' she told him nervously, drawing aside the curtains to let in the light.

'Forget it.'

'It won't take me long to find it,' she assured him hastily, edging towards the door.

'I said forget it!' he ordered sharply, his hand snaking out to grip her wrist, and she was pulled down roughly on to the small sofa. She sat there beside him, uncomfortably erect, and in the farthest corner away from him, but her eyes were wide and a little frightened when, for the first time, she saw him light a cigarette and draw the smoke deep into his lungs. For several nerve-racking seconds he smoked in silence, frowning down at the threadbare carpet beneath his expensive shoes, then his brooding glance captured hers as he asked: 'Where do we go from here, Margot?'

She glanced down at her hands clasped so tightly in her lap, and shrugged lightly. 'Back to where we were before your accident, I suppose.'

'I'm damned if I will!' he exploded with a harshness

that made her jump, then he crushed his half-smoked cigarette into the ashtray beside him and caught her chin between his strong fingers, forcing her eyes to meet his once again. 'We can't go back, Margot,' he said. 'Not after the way you looked when you rushed into that ward and found me well enough to stand up on my own two feet.'

'I would have been concerned about anyone else I might have known well who had just been involved in an accident.' She tried to cover up her revealing actions, but those disturbing fingers against her throat were sending delicious little shivers along her receptive nerves, and they were breaking down the barriers she was trying so desperately to uphold between them.

'Would your concern have been so great that you would have looked as though you were close to fainting with relief when you found them alive and well? No, I don't think so,' Jordan answered his own question with a little mocking laugh, bringing his lips closer to the quivering softness of hers. 'Forget your silly prejudices, Margot, and marry me.'

Time hung suspended while his lips hovered with a tantalising invitation above hers, but she dragged herself free, mentally and physically, of the spell he seemed to weave about her, and she left his side to place the width of the room between them.

Through the window she could see children playing barefoot in the street as she herself had done so many times at their age on a Saturday afternoon when her mother had taken a nap. It was such an incredibly normal scene, but there was nothing normal about the storm brewing within her. It was a storm which had lain dormant for many years, but she could no longer control it as she turned from the window to face Jordan.

'Why should you want to marry someone from the other side of town; someone who wasn't worthy enough once to come to the front door of your home?'

Nearly eight years of bitterness was locked up in that question, and Jordan, shocked and incredulous in the face of it, rose to his feet and demanded harshly, 'What in name of Heaven are you talking about?'

'You know very well what I'm talking about,' Margot accused, her hands clenched at her sides, and pain mirrored in her stormy eyes as they held his glance unwaveringly.

'I'd like to say that I do know,' he said, pushing agitated fingers through his dark hair. 'But, heaven help me, I don't, and I think you'd better explain yourself.'

Margot stared at him, trying to judge the level of his sincerity, but his face was expressionless except for those dark eyes probing hers so relentlessly, and, at last, the festering wound within her opened and the painful matter flowed out into words.

'I was seventeen, and you were in your last year at varsity when I was asked one afternoon to deliver a parcel of dresses to your mother, and it was then that you said——' She choked on the memory and tried again. 'When you opened the door and found me there, you walked away and informed your mother sarcastically that it was that kid from the other side of town at the door, and you added that you were surprised she hadn't told me yet that there was a tradesmen's entrance for people like myself.'

'My God!' was all Jordan said for a moment while he digested this information, then his brow cleared slowly. 'So that's what you've held against me all this time.'

'Can you blame me?'

'Not if what you heard was the truth.'

'But it *is* the truth!' she asserted strongly, then she added with a hint of cynicism hovering about her mouth, 'You were obviously unaware of it at the time, but your voice carried into the hall, and I heard every word you said, so don't call me a liar.'

'What else did you hear?'

'I didn't wait to hear more,' she muttered, bitterness rising within her as she recalled that fateful afternoon when she had discovered that her idol had feet of clay.

'Margot . . .' Again those fingers ploughed through his hair as he bridged the gap between them. 'If you hadn't been in such an infernal hurry to leave, you would have realised from the rest of our heated conversation that my sarcasm had been directed at my mother with the intention of hurting *her*—not *you*.'

'Your *mother*?' she questioned incredulously.

'Yes . . . my mother,' he repeated grimly. 'I don't know why I never gave it a thought before, but that argument with her was the cause of my leaving Willowmead, and the reason why I never returned for so many years. I'd reached the stage where I could no longer tolerate her snobbish attitude, nor her desire to dictate whom I should choose as my friends.' He gestured expressively with his hand, then he added: 'That was when you arrived, and what you heard afterwards was most certainly not intended for your ears, least of all had it been my intention to hurt you. I was using you as an example in an effort to make her see reason, but you wouldn't have known, and neither would you have understood it at the time. You were still too young and impressionable.'

'So I became your whip, but I was the one who was hurt in the process of being used,' Margot remarked bitterly, but her bitterness was now watered down with understanding.

'Margot . . .' His fingers caressed her cheek gently and tentatively. 'Forgive me?'

'All this really makes no difference at all,' she told him quietly, turning away from his disturbing touch. 'I'm still the girl from the other side of town who'll never belong in your society entirely.'

'Don't be ridiculous!'

'Look around you, Jordan,' she cried despairingly, gesturing with her hands towards the old-fashioned sofa and chairs, and the almost threadbare carpet at their feet. 'This has been my home since the day I was born, but it's not the kind of home you're accustomed to. Oh, I could perhaps delude myself for a while that a marriage between us would work, but your way of life is too different from mine to ever make such a union a success.'

She buried her quivering face in her hands to hide the hot, humiliating tears which filled her eyes and spilled on to her cheeks, but they trickled through her fingers and fell on to hands which had fastened on to her wrists to expose her white, tortured features.

'This is where the two ways meet and become one, my darling, because I don't intend that anything should come between us ever again.' The air was charged with emotion as he drew her gently towards him, then he murmured those supremely wonderful words, 'I love you, Margot.'

'Oh, Jordan,' she sighed unsteadily through her tears as a wave of incredible joy surged through her. 'It—it isn't possible.'

'What isn't possible?' he demanded softly.

'That—that you could l-love me.'

'Haven't I been making myself embarrassingly obvious lately?'

'No, you—you haven't,' she whispered brokenly, burying her face against his chest when she could no longer sustain his warm, steady glance. 'I knew you wanted me, but I thought—I thought you merely wanted an affair with someone from the wrong side of town; someone you could drop without qualms once you became bored.'

'My dear Margot!' His hands tightened on her shoulders as he held her a little away from him. 'You don't seem to have a very high opinion of me, do you.'

'I'm sorry,' she smiled a little unsteadily, her eyes brimming with tears as she raised them to his. 'Forgive me?'

His thumbs moved in a sensual caress against her throat. 'I'll forgive you anything if you'll give me the opportunity to make you love me a little.'

'You won't need to try very hard,' she whispered, her senses responding to his touch.

'Margot?'

A flame leapt in his eyes and, unable to maintain his fiery glance, she once again buried her face against his broad shoulder. 'I love you, Jordan. I love you so very much, but——'

His arms, like steel bands, were clamped about her waist, cutting off her air supply even before his mouth swooped down to devour hers, and, hovering between agony and ecstasy, Margot gripped his shoulders with her hands and clung helplessly for seemingly endless seconds before he eased his lips from hers and allowed her to breathe freely once more.

'I needed that,' Jordan said apologetically, and she was on the verge of admitting that she had wanted it just as badly when the shadow of an unhappy memory drove the glow of happiness from her face.

'What about Berdine?' she wanted to know.

'Berdine was the bait supplied by my mother in order to trap me into what she considered to be a suitable marriage, but I'd lost interest while we were still in the Swiss Alps,' he smiled faintly. 'Berdine was useful, however, in my efforts to make you jealous, but I finally sent her packing when her possessiveness began to irritate me.'

'Serves you right for all the agonising moments you made me suffer,' she accused, feigning anger, but then an uncomfortable thought crossed her mind. 'Jordan—your mother——'

'Don't trouble yourself about my mother,' he interrupted, his warm, caressing lips against her throat setting her pulses racing. 'I've bought a piece of ground just outside town, and we'll have a house built there some day soon, but until such time as we find ourselves something small and close to the clinic.'

'Oh, Jordan,' Margot sighed against his lips, and for a time neither of them wanted anything except the physical reassurances they were giving each other.

Later, curled up beside him on the small sofa, she lowered her head gently on to his bruised shoulder. This was a little bit of heaven she would not exchange for anything on earth; but freedom to be with him like this without the need to hide her feelings, and knowing that he loved her in return.

'Are you going to make me wait long?' he asked at length as he trailed his lips across her cheek to her ear with devasting effects.

'I worked my last shift at the clinic last night, and I've sold this house, which means I shall have to move out within two weeks. Then there's also that job I found myself in George, and——'

'Let them know you won't be taking that position after all,' he said at once, his hands urgent as they caressed her. 'I'm not waiting longer than a week for you.'

'Darling . . .' she breathed happily, her lips parting as his descended, and for another length of time she came alive to his touch until mounting desire made her draw away from him. 'About your mother . . .' she said again, still a little breathless from his lovemaking.

'She'll never entirely relinquish her peculiar notions, Margot. Accept that fact, and ignore whatever may follow.' His hand was beneath her chin, forcing her face up to his, and what she saw in his eyes made her weaken with love for him. 'It's you and I that count,' he reminded her softly, his lips brushing across her fluttering eyelids. 'Nothing else is of importance.'

'But I know she'll never accept me.'

'Mother will get used to the idea, and once there's a grandchild for her to fuss over——' He paused abruptly, and surprised laughter burst from his lips. 'You're blushing!' he accused with devilment lurking in his eyes.

Her cheeks were flushed, her eyes luminous with love, and as emotions, warm and vibrant, soared through her, she flung her arms about his neck. 'Oh, darling, darling, hold me close and help me to believe this is true.'

'It *is* true, my beloved,' he assured her, kissing her hard and satisfyingly on the mouth before he buried his face against the softness of her throat. 'I've been going slowly out of my mind these past weeks at the thought of never having the opportunity to make you care just a little, and I was beginning to despair that I would ever make you change your mind about marrying me.'

'Is that why you've been so distracted in the theatre lately?'

Her question made him raise his head sharply to look down into her eyes with a look of incredulity on his face. 'How do you know about that?'

'Daniel spoke to me about it this morning,' she smiled mischievously. 'He practically ordered me to set things right between us, or he would have had to ask for your resignation.'

'Did he really?' Jordan asked, his eyes glittering with laughter. 'Something tells me our Chief Surgeon has enjoyed playing Cupid.'

It was Margot's turn to stare at him incredulously. 'You mean it wasn't as bad as he led me to believe?'

'It was bad enough,' Jordan admitted with a grimace, 'but not to the point where my work actually suffered.'

'Hm . . .' she frowned thoughtfully, 'I think I'm also beginning to understand now why he misled me about your condition when I met him coming out of your ward.'

'It worked, though, didn't it?'

'Jordan . . .' The anxiety of those moments returned to haunt her, and she paled visibly as an anxiety of a different kind swept through her mind. 'Jordan, are you sure?'

'About us, you mean?' he asked with remarkable understanding and, when she nodded, he said roughly, 'I've never been more sure of anything else in my life.' His lips brushed hers with infinite tenderness, exciting her with the promise of more to come. 'There's no going back, Margot. From now on the paths of our lives will run alongside each other as one, and there'll be no more arguments about that.'

'Who's arguing?' she asked teasingly mere seconds before his mouth descended to crush hers into submission, and her lips parted with a hungry yearning she no longer tried to deny. She wanted this man as much as he wanted her, and no one, not even his mother, would be allowed to spoil what they would have together.

Eva Merrick was a proud, autocratic old lady who did not hesitate to speak her mind, but she had lost a great deal of her haughtiness when she called on Margot two days later, and although Margot viewed this visitation with a certain amount of trepidation, she somehow sensed that this woman was no longer her enemy. There was a certain wariness in her manner that evoked Margot's sympathy and, feeling this way, she was aware of the difficulties Eva Merrick was experiencing in conquering her proud, prejudiced nature.

'Could I make you a cup of tea, Mrs Merrick?' Margot asked politely when they sat facing each other in the lounge.

'No, thank you,' Eva Merrick declined with equal politeness.

An awkward little silence followed while they summed each other up mentally, then Margot gently broached the subject which was foremost in their minds.

'I gather Jordan has told you that I've agreed to marry him?'

Eva Merrick stared hard at Margot for a moment, then she nodded her regal head. 'He has,' she admitted.

'I know how you must feel, Mrs Merrick,' Margot said at once with a sympathetic understanding she had never imagined she would feel towards this woman. 'You haven't much of an opinion of me, I know.'

A lace handkerchief fluttered between those slender, remarkably smooth hands, and Margot was surprised to notice that Eva Merrick was having obvious difficulty in controlling her rigid features when she said bluntly, 'I've been a very foolish old woman.'

This concession startled Margot with its unexpectedness. 'Mrs Merrick, I——'

'Let me finish, please,' the older woman interrupted in her usual autocratic manner. 'I'm not finding this easy, as you must know, and I would like to get it off my chest as soon as possible.'

'I'm sorry,' Margot murmured apologetically, feeling very much like a child who had been rapped across the knuckles.

'I've had plenty of time to think since my stay in hospital,' Eva Merrick continued, 'and I realise that I have totally misjudged you. You may not have the wealth and status in life which I have always considered so important, but you have strength of character, and tremendous courage. You have compassion too, I saw it in your eyes that morning before you were discharged from hospital, and I see it now. What more worthy qualities, I wonder, could a mother wish for in the woman her son chooses to marry?'

'Mrs Merrick, I——'

'I'm a difficult woman to please,' Eva Merrick continued as if Margot had not spoken, 'and I warn you that I shall not change in this respect, but I would like to apologise for my rude, insensitive behaviour, and I hope you will have the grace to forgive me.'

Overwhelmed, but with deep sincerity, Margot said: 'To forgive, Mrs Merrick, one must understand, and I would like to think that I do.'

That lace handkerchief fluttered once more, but this

time it actually dabbed at a hint of moisture in those grey eyes surveying Margot without their usual rancour. 'You're very generous.'

'I love Jordan, Mrs Merrick, and, with your help, I would like to make him happy.'

'I shall do my best,' Eva Merrick announced and, as they smiled at each other, Margot had the feeling that a great weight had been lifted from her shoulders to make her happiness complete.

Margot and Jordan were married quietly a week later in the village church with only his mother and their closest friends, Daniel and Joanne Grant, present at the ceremony, and that night, as she lay in Jordan's arms in the main bedroom of the small cottage they had acquired at such speed, he asked softly, 'No regrets?'

'Only one,' she told him, her lips moving against his warm throat. 'I wish my mother could have been here to share this day with us. She liked you very much, and I know she would have been thrilled at the idea of having you for a son-in-law.'

'Your mother knew how I felt about you,' he said, his mouth finding hers in the darkness with a sensuality that never failed to arouse her. 'I made my intentions quite clear when I called on her that afternoon to ask for her assistance in persuading you to dine with me.'

Margot drew away from him a little incredulously. 'You loved me then already?'

'If I have to be absolutely truthful,' he laughed shortly, 'then I think you crept into my heart that day when we collided at school. I dried your tears and bathed your grazed knee, but my heart got a bruise from which it never quite recovered.'

'Oh, Jordan,' she sighed happily against his shoulder.

'I adored you as a child, but I love you now as a woman.'

His lips and arms were a haven from which she had no desire to escape, but her mind conjured up something that had been left unexplained.

'You told me once that you couldn't attend your father's funeral because of someone named Helga,' she began tentatively. 'Did you love her once?'

'I respected and admired Helga Schiller very much,' he explained quietly. 'She was a brilliant pathologist, and the wife of a very good friend of mine. She died of a virus infection for which there was no cure, and I agreed to take over Siegfried's duties in the theatre while he spent those last few days at his wife's bedside.'

'I'm sorry,' she said inadequately, despising herself for having jumped to the wrong conclusion about this woman.

'I love you, Margot,' he groaned, tightening his arms about her as if he were afraid she might try to escape. 'I shall always love you, and in every possible way,' he assured her hoarsely, his lips straying across her throat and down to the swell of her breast. 'Do you think you'll be able to take a lot of loving in large quantities?'

'Try me,' she whispered brokenly, her desire mounting to match his until she was transported once more to those dizzy, ecstatic heights that left her fulfilled and drowsily content in the arms of the man who had chosen her to share his life with him.

The paths of their lives had come together at last in the best possible way. The *only* way!

# Take these
## 4 best-selling novels

# FREE

Yes! Four sophisticated,
contemporary love stories
by four world-famous
authors of romance
FREE, as your
introduction to the Harlequin Presents
subscription plan. Thrill to **Anne Mather**'s
passionate story BORN OUT OF LOVE, set
in the Caribbean.... Travel to darkest Africa
in **Violet Winspear**'s TIME OF THE TEMPTRESS....Let
**Charlotte Lamb** take you to the fascinating world of London's
Fleet Street in MAN'S WORLD .... Discover beautiful Greece in
**Sally Wentworth**'s moving romance SAY HELLO TO YESTERDAY.

*The very finest
in romance fiction*

Join the millions of avid Harlequin readers all over the
world who delight in the magic of a really exciting novel.
EIGHT great NEW titles published EACH MONTH!
Each month you will get to know exciting, interesting,
true-to-life people . . . . You'll be swept to distant lands you've
dreamed of visiting . . . . Intrigue, adventure, romance, and
the destiny of many lives will thrill you through each
Harlequin Presents novel.

*Get all the latest books before they're sold out!*
As a Harlequin subscriber you actually receive your
personal copies of the latest Presents novels immediately
after they come off the press, so you're sure of getting all
8 each month.

*Cancel your subscription whenever you wish!*
You don't have to buy any minimum number of books.
Whenever you decide to stop your subscription just let us
know and we'll cancel all further shipments.